Marin Nelson
118 Falcon St

Frensburg NY

Papa's
Daughter

Books by Thyra Ferré Bjorn

PAPA'S WIFE

PAPA'S DAUGHTER

Papa's Daughter

~~~

THYRA FERRÉ BJORN

~

NEW YORK   Rinehart & Company, Inc.   TORONTO

PUBLISHED SIMULTANEOUSLY IN CANADA BY
CLARKE, IRWIN & COMPANY, LTD., TORONTO

© 1958 BY THYRA FERRÉ BJORN
PRINTED IN THE UNITED STATES OF AMERICA
LIBRARY OF CONGRESS CATALOG NUMBER: 58–6258

To Bob

with

All My Love

Close to the small white church house stood the peaceful-looking parsonage with its neatly raked sand-yard and thick, velvety green grass-carpet where bushes and trees grew in wild profusion. No one would ever suspect that the elderly parson who lived here with his young wife had eight lively youngsters. Pontus Franzon was a man of the old school and had his own unique way of profiting by the overactivity of his offspring. Since, in those days, work seemed to be the cure of all evil, he just planted them here and there among the garden patches, keeping the younger ones busy weeding in the rich black dirt and the older ones carrying water from the lake. By strict orders, they were to give a dipperful of water to each little plant on every day when no rain fell.

This parsonage was located in Lapland, the northernmost province of Sweden, where summers were short and nature lavishly tried to make up for it by letting the sun shine both night and day. Winters, on the other hand, were too long and bitterly cold. The snow drifted as high as mountains and remained on the ground until the spring sun began its melting process. Autumns were also dreary and dark, as black as the ore-mines from which most of the men earned their daily bread. But as if in compensation for the cold and dark, this province possessed a strange wild beauty. When the waterfalls, freed from their ice chains, thundered into broad rivers where salmon jumped and huge logs bobbed in the swift waters, the long winters were forgotten. Then the inhabitants looked with joy for the coming of the season of flame-tinted skies and never-setting sun. This would bring countless numbers of tourists into the village to behold the miracle of the midnight sun.

Inside the parsonage, Pastor Franzon ruled his family according to the Bible and expected each member to grow in righteousness, honoring his God and country. His wife ruled, too. But her weapons were joy, peace and love. Everyone loved this smiling woman with her wide blue eyes and golden blonde hair.

However, there was not always peace in the red and white parsonage! Charlotta Maria, nicknamed Button, the second child of the Franzons, saw to this. Since no one had consulted her, she could not help that she had been born into this world too close to her brother, Nim. He was only a little over a year old when she arrived, and Papa had not had time to get over the shock of Nim's having been born with red hair.

Button had a pair of lungs that seemed to grow stronger daily and the peaceful nights in the study, when Pastor Franzon meditated on the Word of God, soon became only a memory as his feet grew weary from tramping through the house night after night with the fretful new baby in his arms to keep her from screaming her head off. As Button grew, she increased in naughtiness. As a little girl any *no* would challenge her to do the wrong thing and often Papa would look with despair at Mama and ask, "Whatever will become of this child?"

This story, beginning in Lapland five years after the turn of the century, is of Button Franzon, her life, her beaus and, most particularly, the fulfillment of a special dream. It is made up of facts mixed with fiction and sprinkled with lots of fancies.

CONTENTS

BOOK I

BOOK II

BOOK III

BOOK IV

BOOK I

CHAPTER 1

℘ The Sinner

Button was a sinner, a terrible sinner, but right now, as she lay in her bed under the gay patch-quilt, she chose to ignore the fact. It was much more pleasant to relive the joyous happenings of a very eventful Saturday. Although she had been in bed an hour, sleep would not come to her tonight. Her eyes were bright and wide as they peeked once in a while from under the quilt and fastened upon the tiny stream of light, reflected on the ceiling from the night lamp burning in the hallway. All at once, however, the room was too still; so much so that the silence became almost frightening, making it seem as if all the inhabitants of the parsonage were dead. Now the only sound that Button could hear was the beating of her own heart, which was suddenly pounding louder and louder, faster and faster, as she remembered Papa's sermon of last Sunday. She could even hear his voice and see him as he stood in the pulpit of the church with his right hand stretched out as if for a warning to his congregation, then his fist suddenly banging down on the Bible as he shouted, "As I have admonished you before, I admonish you again, anyone that dies with unforgiven sins is a child of the devil!"

Papa never minced his words, strong as they were. Button shivered a little. Sometimes Papa made terrible statements about the devil. How terrifying the thought that one might die without warning and be carried off by that wicked creature! Button's throat felt hot and dry. She thought that she must be suffocating and perhaps about to die. She sat up in bed. Why, she, Button Franzon, had unforgiven sins! Her heart beat so wildly she was certain her small body could not contain it. She was terribly afraid. Maybe at times she had flippantly thought that if some of those stuffy, self-righteous members of Papa's church went to heaven, she certainly wouldn't want to go there, but it would be better than to be carried off by the devil.

Button could no longer breathe; surely she was about to die. Perhaps the devil was lurking somewhere in this room ready to fetch her right now. Her heart hammered louder and louder. She knew the devil couldn't be seen until after death but she knew, just the same, exactly how he looked. No one had actually described him to her, but she had formed her own picture from listening to Papa's sermons. The devil was about four feet tall with a dark slimy body and horns that looked like two sawed-off swords. But it was the tail that conjured up the worst picture of all, for it was long, narrow as a rope, with a sharp pointed end, burning with a fire from the very pit of hell. The claws were sharp and reached out to fetch, and grab and hurt. . . . Perspiration formed on Button's forehead. To be captured by the devil would be the worst thing that could ever happen to anyone. She must get Papa quickly so she could confess her sins. She opened her mouth to cry out to him but not a sound would come; her voice was lost in her fears; she couldn't make it work.

Button knew that of the eight children in the parsonage she had the gift of yelling the loudest. There had been times when Papa even had to take special precautions when he administered his laying on of hands so that the neighbors would not hear the screaming or they would have accused the pastor of torturing his own flesh and blood. Yes, she had the ability to scream so loud that Papa could never punish her very long, so her gift had after all worked out to her advantage. But now Button was lying there soundless and unable to move from fright. Presently the Sabbath stillness of the parsonage was broken by a long eerie scream, for with a final desperate effort Button had at last found her voice. A few seconds later she could hear the footfalls of Mama hurrying to her side.

"What in the world, darling," cried Mama, looking down at her daughter with anxious eyes. "Did you have a nightmare? Are you ill? Does it hurt somewhere?"

Button sobbed loudly. "Yes, Mama, I am sick in here." She pointed to her heart. "I am wicked for I have sinned, and I thought for sure I was going to die, and the devil was right here in the room ready to grab me."

"Hush, child, such foolish talk. How could there be a devil in the parsonage! Turn over now and go to sleep like a good girl."

"No, no, Mama. I want Papa. I want to confess. . . . I . . . I . . ."

Before Mama had time to answer, there stood Papa beside the bed, tall and straight and severe, looking through her as though he wanted to uncover all her sins in one sweeping glance.

"What is all this disturbance, Button?" stormed Papa.

Button gave Mama one last desperate look, but Mama,

knowing very well what the outcome would be, smiled
tenderly down on her and then softly left the room.

"Oh, Papa, Papa," sobbed Button, "I have sinned and
I want to confess so the devil won't get me if I should die."

Papa came nearer the bed. "What have you done, Button?" he asked in a stern voice.

"I stole."

"You what?"

"Yes, it is true, Papa. I stole pennies from Mrs. Lindberg's purse."

For a long moment Papa just stared at Button incredu-
lously. "I can't believe that I'm hearing right," he moaned.

The tears that rolled down Button's face became a
torrent.

"I'm confessing the whole truth, Papa. When Mama
took me with her to visit the sick this afternoon, she left me
in Mrs. Lindberg's room while she and Mrs. Lindberg
went in to pray with Lovisa, who is soon to be breathing
her last breath. You know Lovisa is almost stone deaf and
Mama had to pray very loud to make her hear, and as she
did I just happened to see Mrs. Lindberg's purse lying on
the bed half open and without intending to I opened it a
little more and, Papa, five pennies just rolled into my hand.
I wanted the pennies to buy a chocolate fish—one of the
ones in Rydberg's store window—the one with cream filling—I think it is French cream filling, Papa. I only wanted
one chocolate fish."

Papa started walking back and forth in the small
room.

"And to think," he said, "that there I stand, Sunday
after Sunday. I, the village pastor—I stand there and preach,
asking people to live godly lives and my own daughter who

is not yet ten years old steals money. Yes, to make it worse, she steals from very poor people who live in the poorhouse so she can eat chocolate fishes with cream filling . . . my own daughter a common thief."

"Don't say those awful words, Papa. Don't you even think that I can be forgiven? Do I have to go to hell like Mr. Anderson who murdered his housekeeper?"

"Have you prayed?" snapped Papa.

"Yes . . . no . . . I mean I prayed when I took those pennies . . . I prayed I would not take them. . . . But I did anyway. . . . Prayers just don't seem to work for me."

"Get up and pray," commanded Papa.

Button obeyed. She felt very small as she stood on the cold floor in her long nightie. Papa pointed down and Button knelt. Papa knelt beside her and prayed first, a short prayer but to the point. Button's voice was very small and her prayer came between heartbreaking sobs. . . .

It seemed to her as if the two of them had been kneeling for hours. Her knees were sore, her back ached and she was shivering from head to toe. Finally, everything was very still within her. Her heart was beating normally again and felt clean once more.

"Papa," she whispered, "I think I am forgiven."

"I am sure you are, Button," said Papa kindly. They rose from their knees. "It is now as if it had never been. You are white and clean. Promise me you will never do a thing like that again."

"I promise, Papa. Never, never, as long as I live!"

"That is very fine, my child."

Button crept back into her bed and Papa tucked her in. He wiped her tears with his big handkerchief. "And

now, my dear," he said firmly, "you realize what as a godly
parent I am compelled to do."

Button stared wildly at Papa. "Oh, no," she cried. "Not
this time, Papa. I thought I was all forgiven. You said I was
clean and all white inside. . . ."

But Papa had already departed for the kitchen and
right there on the *kåpa* sat the twig he used for dark of-
fenses.

If Button had taken hope, thinking Papa's kindness
would interfere with his strictness, she had been mistaken,
for he carried out his mission of punishment with just one
thought in mind—that his daughter should know "sin does
not pay."

"If I had neglected to do this, Button," he said before
he kissed her good night, "I'm sure you would very soon
have been thinking of those chocolate fishes in Rydberg's
window again."

Then Button was alone in the dark once more, but
she felt neither anger nor resentment as her tears flowed
freely and she rubbed a very sore spot where the twig had
hit the hardest. She was thoroughly chastened, but she
knew, too, that she had been forgiven. Papa certainly knew
how to handle a sinner, and there was no more fear of the
devil in her thoughts that night.

Button Franzon kept her promise to her Papa, for even
chocolate fishes did not seem so tempting when she remembered what she had had to suffer for them. She sincerely hoped that she would never be tempted to borrow
money from anyone's purse again, with God's help, of
course. But it did not take Button long to forget that she
had chosen to tread the straight and narrow path, and soon

she was entangled in a different type of sinning. It had started out to be only a hilariously funny joke she chose to play on Papa, but she realized, alas, too late that the ladies to whom she told her tale believed it to be the gospel truth.

It was the night of the church family-party and Button had been privileged to sit with Miss Lilja, her schoolteacher, and Mrs. Lund, the head deacon's wife. The conversation had been scintillating and gay. There had been much fooling and laughter until the two ladies began to discuss Pastor Franzon.

"We have, beyond a doubt, the most handsome pastor for miles around," said Miss Lilja, looking across the room to where Papa was sitting.

Button beamed. It was pleasant to have her Papa the topic of discussion. "Yes, Papa is very good-looking," she admitted, blushing a little.

"And, do you know, I believe that if he didn't have that thick mustache, he would look younger than his years," chimed in Mrs. Lund.

Button swallowed hard a couple of times, and then that awful lie came rushing out without any warning. Tears even gathered in her eyes. "Papa *has* to have that mustache to cover his lip, Miss Lilja and Mrs. Lund. . . . Oh, I shouldn't have told you perhaps—no one outside the family knows about it."

"His lip?" asked both the ladies at the same time.

Button with her eyes of summer-sky blue looked very innocent. "Yes, it is deformed—very deformed. He could never have been a preacher if it hadn't been for his mustache. No one would be able to look at him as he preached."

Miss Lilja's mouth opened wide. "Well, of all things! Who would ever believe that our pastor is so skillfully hiding some thing so hideous under a beautiful mustache."

Mrs. Lund looked disturbed. "Child," she said seriously as she looked into Button's eyes, "don't you ever tell anyone else. I'm sure your Papa would be very angry. Do you realize what would happen if the congregation ever got hold of that information? Miss Lilja and I, of course, you can depend upon not to tell a soul."

Button shook her head. Now what had she done! Certainly she had not intended to hurt Papa in any way. For a moment she felt contrite and thought perhaps she ought to tell them she had manufactured the whole thing out of a very imaginative mind, but the two ladies were walking away, looking as if they had inherited a gold mine, so why should she lose her status of importance? After all, there was little chance that Papa would ever know, and he would never shave off his mustache . . . she hoped. And wasn't the important thing that his upper lip *was* as normal as anyone's?

If Button had stopped with that experience, she would have saved herself and others a lot of grief. Unfortunately, she loved excitement and did not always wait to reason whether a thing was good or bad. When the story about Papa's lip had died down, she again took a step in the wrong direction, and as before the two prominent ladies helped feed fuel to the fire.

This time it was Miss Larson they had chosen for a subject. Stina Larson was a shy, lonesome-looking lady, but she managed to do more hard work in the Lord's Vineyard than all the others put together.

"We must do something very special for her, Ingrid," said Mrs. Lund to Miss Lilja, just as Button happened to pass them in church.

"A splendid idea, Mia *lilla*," smiled Miss Lilja. "Wouldn't it be nice to give her a party at an appropriate time?"

"Miss Larson is my Sunday-school teacher," Button informed them proudly, "and I heard what you were just saying about a party." Then, before she had time to stop herself, words out of nowhere came rushing to her tongue again. "She has a birthday next week—a real big one—she will be fifty!"

"Fifty!" exclaimed Mrs. Lund. "Who ever would have believed that a little mouse like that would hide fifty years behind that calm face of hers. But what a chance! I'll talk to Pastor Franzon and the other ladies and we'll make plans for a big celebration. . . . You just wait and see! And thanks a lot to you, Button *lilla*."

A few days later a committee of ladies were busy making plans. According to Swedish custom, special birthdays called for special doings and, since the fiftieth birthday was the greatest of them all, it called for singing outside the lucky person's window early in the morning. Afterwards, of course, there was the usual coffee in bed, the gifts and speeches. It seemed that everyone wanted to remember Miss Larson and fifty *kronor* were collected and placed in a large envelope for Papa to present to her. As far as the church people knew, Miss Larson had no relatives and no one, not even Papa, who had the birthdays of all his members recorded, had thought of checking up on Button's statement. Since Mrs. Lund had been the one to approach Papa concerning the affair, Papa naturally took it for granted that she had correct facts.

On the eventful morning Button was surprised to be

awakened at four thirty. She had not counted on being invited to this party of grownups. Miss Lilja, however, had called late the previous evening and suggested that Button should be permitted to attend the party. "After all," she told Mama, "if Button hadn't been so kind as to tell us it was Stina's birthday, we never would have known."

Mama touched Button's cheek lightly and whispered in her ear, "Get up, my dear. Miss Lilja wants you to join us in Miss Larson's singing-party. Hurry now, so we won't be late."

Button rubbed her sleepy eyes and dressed quickly. Something as sharp as a sewing needle was pricking her conscience. How had she ever gotten into this predicament? And how would Miss Larson take it? Would she remain silent and pretend that it was her birthday, or would she be very angry? Button wondered how old she really was. It was too late now to stop the festivities, so she would just keep quiet and hope for the best.

Presently she was standing with the rest of the people below Miss Larson's bedroom window. Her heart beat wildly. If she could only escape, but there was no place to go without being seen. There was Mr. Groth with his violin, Peter Janson with his guitar, and Erik Lund with his flute. Exactly at five o'clock the musicians struck a chord loud enough to awaken the dead, and the whole group started to sing a hymn at the top of their voices from the songbooks Papa had brought in Torkel's wagon. "'A morning without sin we shall awake,'" rang out the happy chorus.

The song had five verses, and when they came to the second line of the fourth verse, the window flew open and Miss Larson, sleepy-eyed and with curlers in her hair, gazed down at the singing people as if she were still dreaming.

"Congratulations! . . . Happy birthday! . . . God bless Stina!" echoed the voices from below. But Stina Larson just stood there staring as if she had frozen into a statue.

"Open the door, Stina *lilla*," cried Mama, "The coffeepot is getting chilly."

Miss Larson unbolted the door, and in trotted the whole congregation of friends and co-workers. A slightly dazed Miss Larson was served coffee in bed on a big silver tray, and cups were passed to all the celebrants. If the party were to be judged by what the ladies had brought for refreshments, it certainly was a success. There were fancy cookies and coffee breads galore, and a huge cake on which was written, STINA LARSON 50 YEARS.

Miss Larson, who had still not said a word, was stirring her coffee nervously and nibbling on a cookie.

After Papa had had his coffee, he made an excellent speech, telling of Miss Larson's faithfulness and finally ending with:

"You have reached fifty now and stand on the very top of the circle of life. From now on, Stina, you will slowly descend, year by year, step by step . . ." and Papa put in so many pretty words that it brought tears to some of the ladies' eyes and Mr. Groth had to blow his nose hard. Others spoke after this and then the gifts—the flowers and the money—were presented.

Finally it was Miss Larson's turn. She sat up in bed, pillows propped at her back, her cheeks flushed as red as roses, her eyes gleaming strangely, and her mouth held as if she were trying hard to keep from crying.

Mama leaned over her. "You'd better give us a few words, Stina," she said, and sat down on the bed beside her.

But Miss Larson could no longer control herself. She threw herself into Mama's arms and sobbed as if her heart would break.

"There, now," soothed Mama gently. "We all get over-excited at a surprise party like this. I remember the last time you surprised me! I thought I'd just fall into a heap and die! You'll feel better in a few minutes . . . just remember we are your friends."

Bravely Stina Larson lifted her head and tried to speak. "*Pastorn* . . . Maria . . . friends . . . all of you kind people. . . . I know you are sweet—and wonderful—and well-meaning. . . . I—I . . ." But a fresh flood of tears stopped her.

"We all understand the depths of your feelings, Stina," Mama whispered. "Go ahead and cry if it will make you feel better."

Miss Larson was soon composed again. She wiped her eyes with the sleeve of her nightgown. "That's the worst of it . . . I can't understand any of this. . . . That's why I'm crying. Since you are all my friends, why are you playing this joke on me? Why are you waking me up early in the morning with song, coffee, speeches, gifts and a birth-day cake when it is not my birthday. . . . And why in the world do you make me fifty years old when I am only forty-one!"

It was exceedingly quiet in the bedroom. No one dared to move or speak. All eyes were fixed upon Papa as if he would have the answer to this riddle. Button, who had been sitting unnoticed by the door, decided it was time to disap-pear, but this act helped her for a moment only. . . .

Later that morning, before she could go to school, she had to face Mama and Papa. That telling lies was as sinful as stealing pennies was a lesson Papa was determined to teach his child. Not even Mama, who was still shocked at her daughter's capacity to make up untrue stories, would interfere, but gave Papa a free hand. As a result, Button lost all desire to tell falsehoods. Even though they gave her a temporary sense of importance, it was not worth while. And both Mama and Papa desperately hoped that this time she had really learned her lesson.

She had not. A few weeks later she was thrown into another situation that was to have a great influence on her life. This time it was because of her fascination for words. Not nice words such as the people in Papa's church and the inhabitants of the parsonage spoke. No, these were words that were taboo among all Button's playmates and that she never heard spoken in her daily life. Button was curious by nature, and her ears seemed to be sharper than those of other children, so that they heard and picked up what they were not supposed to hear.

In the village lived a brewer, Sandquist by name, who, everyone knew, drank like a fish. When he was in his cups, he often chased his wife down the street until she found refuge with some of her friends, who would keep her until he was sober once again.

Button had never witnessed one of these scenes until one night when Papa had written a very important letter to the Conference and had asked Button to mail it for him. As she was walking down the street, a couple suddenly ran past her so swiftly that, if it had not been for the stream of words Mr. Sandquist had let out, she would have thought she had just imagined it. Mr. Sandquist had a stick in one hand and a bottle in the other, and the words he hurled after his wife stuck in Button's mind. She had stood there staring as if she could not believe either her eyes or ears. If Sandquist had not been such a prominent political figure, or had not had such an amount of money, he surely would have landed in the jail outside the village limit. But everybody excused him because his name was Sandquist and also because they knew that, when brewer Sandquist was sober again, he would deeply regret his sins and ask his wife's forgiveness on bended knee; he would buy her candy and flowers and be the sorriest man ever, until he fell again.

Button had been awestruck. But when she went to her room that night, she marked down the strange words she had heard under the title, WORDS UNKNOWN TO BUTTON FRANZON. The next day she took them to school and showed them to her best friend, Karin Lund.

"Button," cried Karin, staring down at Button's paper, "why, those are nasty swear words! You ought to be ashamed to carry them with you. . . . What if your Papa saw them?"

"I'm not saying them, Karin, not even thinking them—just keeping them. . . . It can't be a sin to do that."

"Although I'm just a deacon's daughter, I'd never dare to keep them," exclaimed Karin, her eyes almost popping out of her head as she continued to look over Button's shoulder at the paper. "But *I* know a man that says even worse words than those. He is a tramp and lives in an old shack beside the railroad. That man even swears those words when he is alone. I bet he even says them in his sleep. Old man Lot, I have heard my Mama say, is the world's champion swearer."

"Karin," said Button, "do you think we could go down and listen to him?"

"What for?"

"I want more words. . . . I'm collecting them."

Karin looked horrified. "Why, may I ask, Button Franzon?"

"I'm going to sell them for pennies, or hair ribbons, or pencils, or I may perhaps even get a rabbit's foot. . . . I'll give you half of everything I get, if you go with me to listen to the old man by the tracks."

"We—ll . . . I'll see," promised Karin. "I'll tell you after school."

That afternoon two little girls with yellow pigtails made their way across the field to the railroad tracks. Each was equipped with paper and pencil and could have passed for a miniature news reporter. They were in luck. The old man sat sleeping with his head against the wall outside the shack. He was dirty and unkempt. An old pipe hung from his bearded mouth. The yard, littered with beer bottles and tin cans, was as dirty as the old man. A few chickens strutted around, trying to scratch in the hard dirt. A pig rolled in a filthy sty. The whole place smelled foul. The girls hid behind a bush. A mosquito landed on the old man's forehead. It woke him up and started a bombardment of strange words. The pipe fell from his mouth and landed in a puddle, and that gave Button more words than she had time to write down. Soon the man slept again and the girls made their getaway.

"Did you ever hear anything like it?" asked Button.

"I wonder if there is *one* naughty word that man doesn't know!" said Karin. Their feet were almost at running speed now, and Karin looked a bit frightened. "Don't you ever, ever tell your Papa I took you there."

"I won't," replied Button. She was wondering how she

would remember all those words she had not had time to write down.

The next day a lot of secret whispers were going around the school, and the two girls had no trouble selling all the word lists they had had time to make up. Those unfortunates that could not buy a list found ways in which they could borrow one and commit the words to memory.

Miss Lilja, who had not been entirely blind to the goings-on in her classroom, started an investigation to find the instigator of these whisperings and note-passings. One boy, who had been unable to purchase a list, supplied her with the needed information, but when Miss Lilja saw a list of the words, she stared at it in utter amazement. Feeling the problem too big for her to cope with herself, she decided to ask the pastor if he would come in and speak to the children concerning the second commandment. The next day Papa came and, when he was through speaking, there wasn't a child whose head was not bowed in shame. Many raised their hands in solemn promise that they would never become involved with swear words again.

"There is only one way, though," concluded Papa, "that the school can be washed clean of the stigma that has been put upon it. Evil always has a beginning. Who started this? I shall return to this school at one o'clock tomorrow afternoon and expect to find the culprit waiting for me in Miss Lilja's office."

Deeply frightened that her Papa would hear about this, Karin went to Miss Lilja and told her the whole story. She begged Miss Lilja not to let Button know that she had informed on her.

The next afternoon Miss Lilja simply called Button's name. "I want you, Charlotta, to go to my office and be waiting there when Pastor Franzon arrives," she told the surprised Button. "He will thereby know that you are the one to whom he is to speak."

Button gasped. She wondered how Miss Lilja had found out that she was the guilty one. There was nothing to do now but to face whatever happened, Button thought, as she walked with slow steps down the long corridor and through a door marked *Office*.

Once inside the office, all the bravery seemed to leave her, and the minutes passed by as slowly as if they were hours before she heard Papa's footsteps coming down the hall. As he opened the door, she fixed her eyes on the worn spot in the gray rug in front of the desk. Papa shut the door and Button realized that by now he knew the worst. She waited for the storm to break loose, but there was nothing save a heavy silence as if thick fog had settled over the world. Minutes ticked away on the big round clock on the wall, but still not a sound from Papa. Then Button lifted her eyes, her legs trembling under her. She looked straight into Papa's blue eyes and at first she could not believe what she saw. There was no anger written there, no condemnation, only sorrow and compassion. Her own eyes grew wide. Was that her Papa who had eyes like that, so filled with tender love? They looked like sorrowing stars lost in the night. A strange light gleamed in them. Presently two big tears spilled over and rolled down his cheek. Without one word to her he turned and walked out, closing the door gently behind him.

Button felt like rushing after him, throwing herself into his arms and telling him she was ashamed and broken-hearted and so sorry. She would do anything in the world to make things right again. Anything! Because she loved him with all her heart. But only her heart went after him; her feet could not move. They felt as if they were made of cast iron. She did not know how long it was before she slowly returned to her classroom.

The sadness would not leave Button's heart, which seemed to swell out and embrace all of her. The lists had been gathered and burned in the wood stove in the classroom. Miss Lilja, with tears running down her cheeks, had prayed the Lord's Prayer with the class. Button spoke the words, too, saying them very sincerely: "and forgive us our trespasses."

She walked home alone and spoke to no one. She was conscious of nothing but that look in Papa's eyes. If she had been punished for a week, she could not have felt more chastened. Papa and Mama were very silent during the evening meal, but Button noticed that her slice of cake was bigger than the others. After dinner her brother Nim volunteered to help with the dishes in her place, so Button studied her lessons, then bade everyone good night. Everything seemed so unreal, as if she were moving in a dream. She had lost all desire to be naughty. She knew she would never deliberately or thoughtlessly hurt Papa again.

She did not go to sleep readily and when she finally did, something prompted her to wake up. She stirred restlessly. Suddenly she made her way to the master bedroom. The snores told her both Papa and Mama were asleep. She stood there looking down at them for a few moments. She was a big girl now, almost ten years old. She had been a problem to Papa, and though he had tried to whip the badness out of her, it had never worked. But what his hands had not been able to accomplish—his eyes had. The love in them and the two tears had cured her.

"Papa," Button whispered, touching him gently on the shoulder.

He opened his eyes and looked up at her.

"Button," he said and opened his arms. "I knew you would come to me."

Button nestled close in his arms. "I wanted to tell you that I am more sorry than I have ever been. I don't know why I do those naughty things, Papa, but I have asked God to help me be good. I think He will."

Papa kissed her tenderly. "He surely will, Button, and when a sinner repents, even though she be but a very young girl, all the bells in heaven ring with joy."

Button could almost hear those bells as she glanced out at the night sky on the way to her room. Surely the whole world was rejoicing in the fact that she wanted to be good.

CHAPTER 2

❧ The Call

What a wonderful Monday! Strange! This was contrary to what Mondays were supposed to be in the parsonage, for to Papa and Mama they were "blue" days. Button wondered why Mondays should be different from any other day in the week. Hadn't God made seven days, each one lovely and beautiful, each morning filled with breathless anticipation of what it might bring? But, no, Mama had to explain, this was not so when one lived in the parsonage. Then Mondays were "blue," a letdown from the rush and excitement of Sunday when a pastor had to be at his best, preaching, singing, smiling, shaking hands with all the people, and his wife had to use up her spare energy trying to make the children behave in the manner expected of them by the church people and not in the uninhibited noisy way they would act without a firm hand to guide them. Even just getting through Saturday was a chore for Mama, since then the house had to be kept hushed as if Papa were a bachelor instead of a married man with eight children. Unless it was quiet around him, Papa couldn't receive those divine inspirations that prompted so many good sermons! By Monday both Papa and Mama were nervously exhausted, but it had to be another day of quiet so Papa could rest, which meant another task for Mama to keep her household running smoothly without confusion. Mama's patience having been spent, she was apt to be a little snappy with the children and not her usual gentle self. Thus "blue" Mondays.

For Button this particular Monday was anything but blue. In the morning Mama had taken out a brand-new white apron for her.

"You mean I can really wear this today, Mama?" cried Button, showing by her radiant eyes the gladness that filled her heart.

"Yes, dear, you might as well," agreed Mama, "because if we save it too long, you will just outgrow it! It's a very pretty one, isn't it?"

"Pretty! Oh, Mama, it is heavenly! Look at the lace ruffles and all the tiny pearl buttons. No one but Tant Renberg would put so much work into a mere apron."

"Tant is a darling. Remember, Button, that this was your Christmas present from her, and when you see her, tell her how happy it has made you."

She stood very still so Mama could button all the buttons on the back of the apron all the way down to the hem. How thankful I am, she thought, to have a lovely apron to cover up my brown dress. Button hated brown . . . mousey . . . dirty . . . colorless brown. She hoped this would be the last brown dress she would ever have to wear. Why couldn't she convince Mama that brown was a most unsuitable color for her, exactly matching those horrid little freckles on her nose? Oh, why did she have to have freckles anyway! She might have been pretty if it hadn't been for these, but no one could be beautiful who had even a speck of a freckle.

Button would be very careful not to get this apron dirty and when she came home from school, she would take it off and hang it upon the apron-nail in the kitchen closet. Then she would put on the apron she had been wearing the week before. This new one would be turned inside out in the middle of the week so it would look clean again for the rest of the week. Since the family wash was done only twice a year, even a little girl had to be careful not to get clothes soiled.

Button skipped and danced along the way to school. It was spring and the world was going to look new and alive very soon. The long, long winter was gone at last. At the top of the hill, by the bend in the road, she saw Karin waiting for her.

"Why Button Franzon, I hardly recognized you," she cried. "You look like an eloping bride. What a gorgeous apron!"

"Tant Renberg made it for me and gave it to me for Christmas," replied Button nonchalantly, her head high. "This is the first time I've worn it."

"I wish I were a preacher's child. No one would ever think to make such an apron for a deacon's daughter!"

At school all the girls gathered around Button to admire her new apron. They felt of it, examined the tiny buttons, and agreed that it was a most beautiful gift. When class began, Button noticed that Miss Lilja looked her way over and over again. Button was sure that she, too, was fascinated by the lovely white apron. But it wasn't until midmorning that the teacher said, "Charlotta Franzon, you look so pretty today. Will you come to the front of the room and read to the class?"

Button felt her heart beating fast with joy. It was a wonderful day! In spite of her freckles, the teacher must think that she was beautiful, and therefore was honoring her by letting her be the reader of the day. She walked quickly to the front of the room and stood very poised before Miss Lilja's desk and read from the thick, gray lesson book the story of Fredrika Bremer, who was a great Swedish-Finnish author and had written a book named *Hertha* as well as many other stories.

On the front page there was a picture of Miss Bremer. Button glanced at it. She would have been a pretty woman, she thought, if she hadn't had such a large nose. Perhaps having freckles wasn't so bad after all. It was better than having a large nose. If she ever became famous, she wanted to be very pretty. Button began to read from her lesson book in a strong, clear voice: "What does a little girl mean to this world? Can even she be great and famous? . . ." At those words of Fredrika Bremer's something stirred deeply within Button. She continued reading for the class, sentence after sentence, but she herself did not know what she was reading, for her whole attention was focused on those opening sentences. They echoed over and over again in her mind. Perhaps Miss Bremer, too, had once stood in front of a class and read and perhaps when she did, she knew that when she grew up, she would write words for others to read—words that would make people smile or sigh, or laugh, or cry. The words burned like fire now. . . . Why not? Even a little girl born in a parsonage could grow up and write words that others would read. Yes, Button knew now that she had received a call from deep within her heart to be a writer. She would not just get married and clean and sew and cook and sweep, wash dishes or have children. . . . She would grow up to write books! She would dress in pretty clothes, sit in a lovely room and write stories and be an author just like Fredrika Bremer. And wouldn't Papa be thrilled when she became famous and other children could read about Charlotta Franzon in their lesson books?

"That is all, Charlotta," said Miss Lilja kindly. "That was very well read. Thank you! You may take your seat now."

But Button was so engrossed in her own thoughts that, instead of taking her seat, she had just stood there like a *dumbom*. . . . Slowly she came out of her reverie, flushed, and walked to her seat beside Karin to the accompaniment of giggles from her classmates.

"You looked so queer, Button, standing there so long," whispered Karin. "Did you think we needed more time to notice your apron?"

"Never mind, Karin. I didn't stand there to show off my apron. I wasn't even conscious of it. You sound envious, which isn't becoming to a deacon's daughter, you know. Something much more exciting happened. I know now what I am going to be when I grow up."

"An author?" asked Karin.

Button stared in surprise. "However did you know?"

"Oh, I was just teasing because you read about one. Are you really?"

Button nodded her head, her pigtails bobbing up and down.

"I bet every child in school will read your books," declared Karin, looking at her classmate as if she had been transformed into a fairy princess.

Button did not answer. She was again lost in deep thoughts, staring straight ahead at the teacher's desk.

When school was over, Button did not wait for Karin as was her usual habit, but hurried off alone toward the mountain road as fast as her legs would go. She must be by herself to think over all these things that had rushed through her mind. She would not help Mama this afternoon. Mama would not be worried about her, for she would surmise that Button had stayed after school to help Miss Lilja straighten up the room. She often enough did this.

She had walked so fast that she was beginning to gasp, so she finally sat down under a big tree on the mountain slope. The leaves were starting to burst their buds, and the spruce trees spread a heavy, balmy springtime perfume through the air. Button leaned against the tree and pressed her cheek against the rough bark. Her eyes felt heavy, and she wanted to close them and dream the beautiful dreams that seemed to be floating through the air in her direction, but she shook off her drowsiness and took a paper and pencil from her schoolbag. If she was to dedicate herself to being an author, she must first find out if she could write.

She wrote a sentence in large upright letters and then stared at it in disgust. "Once upon a time," she had begun. Why, anybody could write that! It showed no special talent at all. She would have to do better than that! She would try again . . . and this time it came!

Button pressed the paper joyfully against her heart, unable to believe that the words written thereon had come so wonderfully and mysteriously from her pencil. Whoever but a real author could think of words like that? It was

strange, she thought, that locked up within herself there
were words that she did not know she possessed . . .
words that would knock on her brain and beg to be let out.
All her storybooks would begin with pretty words such as
these, so that when people read her books, their sadness
would vanish away, for she would make them laugh and
be gay. Under the title she had written she had signed a
new name, Mary Terrier, which also had come from within
her as if it had always existed there. That would be her
new name—her writer name. For a long time only Mama
and Papa and she would know that Button Franzon was a
writer. How pretty the name looked:

Once upon a Lily Pad
by
Mary Terrier

At first she had not intended to tell Mama so soon, but
the thing that filled her felt like a big balloon and by the
time she reached the parsonage, she was sure that unless
she shared her secret with someone she would burst. Mama
was in the kitchen ready to put an *apple-kaka* in the oven.

"Why, Button, such a beaming face!" exclaimed
Mama. "You must have found at least one hundred *kronor*
on your way home from school."

"Better than that, Mama," sang Button jubilantly,
completely ignoring Mama's cooking art. "Mama, I have
just discovered what I shall become when I grow up. I
shall write books like Fredrika Bremer's! I shall be an
author!" Button stopped her flow of words as the importance of the occasion came to her. "Mama, can we talk for a
while in *salen?*"

Mama looked at her daughter in surprise. It was not like Button to talk this way, but if it meant a turn for the better, she was happy. Instead of a headstrong little girl she seemed like a reformed individual. One of these days she might even be able to say to Papa, "Pontus, I think that Button may turn out as well as the other seven children after all."

Mama took her time placing the *apple-kaka* in the oven. She wiped her hands thoroughly on the towel which hung by the stove, and followed Button into the best room of the parsonage. They sat down on the sofa, and Mama playfully placed her arm around Button's shoulders and smiled down on her.

"Now what is on your heart, darling?" she asked.

Not for one moment did Button hesitate. Her cheeks were flushed and her big blue eyes looked wistfully far, far away, out through the window at the mountains towering against the evening sky.

"I shall be a very famous person, Mama. . . . I shall write books, stories and poems, and everybody in the whole of Sweden will know the name of Franzon someday."

Mama drew a sigh of relief. "Was that all you wanted to tell me, Button? For such a young girl to have such fine dreams is commendable. However, I must admit you had me worried for a moment. I thought you wanted to confess some wrong you had committed."

Button opened her mouth to speak, but no words would come. Surely, this couldn't be all it meant to Mama. It seemed as though all of a sudden the sun had ceased to shine.

"Button," said Mama softly, "don't look as if the world had come to an end. I hope that you can write books some-

day, but right now you shouldn't live in a dream. You have
more important things to think of. First, you must learn to
keep house well, for you owe that to the man you will marry
someday. There is much to learn about sewing, cleaning
and cooking, as well as the art of being a good mother. Do
you know, for instance, my little girl, that babies are like
tiny, delicate plants on which you have to bestow love and
tender care in order for them to grow and be strong? Someday you and I will wander deep into the woods and I'll
show you and tell you of the mystery of life. These are the
things with which you should be filling your little heart.
And as for books, you know that Papa is the book-man in
this house. So later, when you feel you are ready to write,
you talk it over with him."

"Thank you, Mama." Button's voice shook a trifle. "I
just wanted to share my secret."

"Button!" Horror was written on Mama's face. "Oh,
Button, my *apple-kaka!* I must have forgotten to turn the
oven down. . . . It smells like burning . . . out of my
way." And Mama ran toward the kitchen as fast as her feet
could carry her.

For a few minutes Button remained still on the davenport, fighting hard to control her tears. Something deep
within her was very bruised. Mama did not understand
about "the call," thinking her just a little silly girl. If the
apple-kaka was burned, she would understand about that
and would blame Button for taking up her time when she
was busy. Little Mama cared that Button had opened the
secretmost place of her heart. She would go to Papa. Papa
would understand about a little girl's dreams. Didn't Papa
understand just about everybody in the whole world?

Since it was Monday, Papa would be in his study resting. Button hesitated a bit outside the heavy door, then with her head held high she pushed it open and stepped inside. "Papa," she said softly, "I have something very important to tell you."

But Papa was not resting! He put down his pencil and closed the big Bible after placing an envelope between its pages. "Button Franzon, what have I told you about walking into my study without knocking on the door first and waiting for an answer? Don't you realize that I could have been praying for a sinner? As it is, I was working on my next Sunday's sermon, and your interruption has made me lose my trend of thought completely. It may never come back to me, and it was one of the best thoughts I have ever had concerning Andrew and the loaves and fishes. Now it is lost not only to me but to the whole congregation as well. Who knows but that that sentence may have saved a soul who will now perish? When you came bursting in like that, I thought that at least the house was on fire or that Mama had fallen down the stairs or some other such calamity. Let me caution you never to repeat this offense or I'll have my own way of dealing with you."

Button backed away from Papa's study. She felt as if her heart would break with the immensity of the hurt, and running to the garden, she put her arms around a tree and cried. Blue Monday! Yes, indeed, it was. But Papa and Mamma had no right to let their emotions affect her life. This had started out to be the most wonderful day she had ever lived and no one had a right to ruin it. She would never share her secrets with her parents again, but would hug them to her heart and keep them to herself. But someday they would see. . . . Button forced a smile and dabbed at her eyes with the corner of her new apron which in her excitement she had forgotten to change. . . . Someday they would know that she had received a real call, and then she would never again need to cry because she was hurt. As for now, she would create within herself a new world where she would dwell and be happy and tomorrow she would begin her first story.

"After all," Button said aloud, "there will always be *apple-kaka* to bake and sinners to pray for, but to receive a call to be an author can only happen once to a little girl not quite ten years old."

The following day, however, Button did not write her story. Karin prevented it. She was waiting for Button at their accustomary meeting place on the way to school. As Button approached, she waved her hand gaily. "Hi there, author!" she called loudly.

Button looked annoyed. "Hush, Karin, don't let anyone hear my secret," she whispered, taking hold of Karin's arm.

"Oh, I didn't think it was a secret. Doesn't anyone else know, really?"

"Well, Mary Terrier, of course."

Karin's eyes grew wide. "Who in the world is Mary Terrier?"

"I am talking about me, it's my pen name. Lots of authors use a different name from their own in order to have privacy until they become famous."

"Gosh, Button, you certainly know an awful lot of things. I promise not to tell a soul, because I'm so proud to share your secret."

With their arms around each other, the two girls wandered on toward the schoolhouse.

"Are you a really, truly author now?" asked Karin unbelievingly.

Button nodded importantly. "I am starting my first story today."

"Please tell me what it's all about?" Karin pressed Button's arm hard and looked pleadingly into her face. "After all, I am your very closest and best friend."

"I know that," laughed Button, feeling herself grow several inches taller. She looked wistfully up at the blue sky. "But I don't know myself yet what I am going to write. You see, when you've been given the talent to write, stories just flow out of your mind easily as soon as you sit down with a paper and pencil. You just couldn't be an author without this special talent."

"Oh, my," responded Karin humbly. "I didn't know all those things, and here I was just about to ask you if I could help you write your stories, but if it's only that talent thing you need, then I guess I'd be useless."

"Whatever gave you the idea that *you* could help?" wondered Button, aloud.

Karin blushed. "Well, you see, there is to be a deacons' meeting at our house tonight and since they discuss all the sins of the church people, I thought perhaps you and I would listen in the big closet in *lille-salen*. . . . and you could get an honest-to-goodness true story to write."

"You are mixing up reporters with authors, Karin. If you work on a newspaper, you take down what people say at a meeting. You don't know anything about writing, do you?"

"I guess not. I just thought, since we were such good friends, that perhaps I could help a little, but I know now that it was just a foolish notion."

But Button had been thinking, and there was subdued excitement in her voice as she said, "Wait a minute, Karin. Maybe you do have a good idea. I can always use my talent on the next story. It might be fun to listen." Button's eyes twinkled at the thought of being an unseen listener at a deacons' meeting. "We will do it, Karin! Thanks for telling me."

"You come along with your Papa, or better yet, come earlier, then my folks will think we are doing lessons in my room. . . ." Karin was warm with excitement as she planned each detail of how they would hide inside the closet and get out unseen after the meeting was over. It was only eight in the morning now, and it seemed like an eternity to have to wait until seven at night. It was even harder to concentrate on schoolwork and now and then the two girls would look at each other and giggle behind their hands as they thought of the things their ears would hear before the day was done.

At six thirty that evening the girls stood hidden behind a thick fur coat in the big closet in Deacon Lund's home. It was warm and stuffy in there and the moth-ball smell made Button want to sneeze so much that she almost pinched her nose off trying to suppress the desire.

"Don't you dare to sneeze, Button. . . . If my Papa caught us in here, you would never live to write the story."

Button wiped her eyes. "I'll do my best, but I do hope the meeting begins soon."

And it did not take long before all the deacons had assembled. Button heard Papa's voice saying that *polka-grisar* was his favorite candy. The girls' mouths were drooling at the thought of Mr. Lund passing around candy, but they could do nothing but keep as still as two little mice so as not to give away the show.

Suddenly Mr. Lund called out, "Have coffee ready for us in an hour, Mia dear!" And a door was shut. It was very still in the room for a moment. Button and Karin pressed their ears against the thin wall and the excitement of it all made Button forget her urge to sneeze. This was the most daring thing she had ever undertaken.

"Brethren"—the meeting had started and Papa's voice came deep and clear—"we shall begin this important meeting by asking the Lord to bless us in all that we say and do that it may be for the good of His church here on earth. Brother Lindgren, will you lead us in prayer?"

"I bet he'll pray for ten minutes, at least. He's the longest pray-er in the church with the exception of Mr. Olauson," whispered Karin.

And she was right. Mr. Lindgren prayed very slowly, repeating his words over and over as if the Lord was slow to understand. Finally he said amen and several other amens testified to the fact that the prayer was ended.

"Brother deacons"—it was Papa's voice again—"I know you are just as sorrowful as I am to find that Deacon Petter Anderson is missing from our midst tonight. It puts me in mind of the Last Supper when Judas Iscariot left the disciples to betray his Lord. Our brother Anderson has fallen again!"

"Is he a painter?" whispered Button.

"Of course not, silly," said Karin in a hushed voice. "Anderson hasn't fallen from a ladder. He has fallen into sin!"

"Oh," said Button, surprised. A deacon's daughter certainly had the advantage of knowing the shortcomings of the church members.

"Pastor Franzon," said Deacon Lund. "We all know of Petter's fall. The temptation has been too much for him. My wife with several of the other ladies saw him staggering down the street last Saturday night."

"See, I told you! He was drunk!" exclaimed Karin triumphantly.

For a while all was quiet outside the closet door. Then the squeaky voice of Aron Kvist was heard to say, "He certainly has no right to be a deacon if he can't let the devil's drink alone."

"I move we strike his name from the church roll," said Lindgren.

"Wait a moment," said Papa. "We must never be too hasty in passing judgment on others. It is said that God does not count sins, He weighs them. Let us examine our own hearts. Have we always behaved as it behooves servants of the Lord?"

Button knew that right now Papa would be looking at each man in the room, and his eyes would pierce through all of them until they feared that he could see all their hidden sins. Button felt sure no one would dare to accuse Anderson again.

Papa was speaking again. "I want to talk to this fallen brother and ask him to join us at our next meeting. Perhaps we can be of help to him. He may be sorry and ask our forgiveness as well as that of God. If that should happen, we must not be a hindrance to him, for with kindness and understanding we may place his feet on the narrow way again."

"I still believe his name should be removed," retorted Lindgren, "for as long as he remains on the board, it will be like having one soiled spot on a clean cloth. What will those outside the church think of us if one of our number is a drunkard? You can't hide this sort of thing. I'm sure that the ladies from our church were not the only ones who saw him stagger."

A long discussion followed, but in the end Papa won out, and the girls were glad because they both liked kind Mr. Anderson but disliked Lindgren. Next came the glad news that Miss Sofia Ringstrom had bequeathed eight hundred *kronor* to the deacon treasury to do with as the deacons saw fit for the growth and furtherance of God's work.

"And now," said Papa, "unfortunately we have some more heartbreaking business. What shall we do with Edith Strom?"

"Is the talk about her true?" asked Deacon Svenson.

"It is," answered Papa in a low voice. "I visited Edith yesterday."

"And your eyes confirmed that the gossip about her is true?" This from Mr. Lund.

"Sadly yes," said Papa. "Whenever she sees her father coming home from work, she escapes into the attic and she stays there whenever he is at the house. She is terrified lest he find her and discover her condition. He thinks she is out of town visiting her sister. She is the most pitiable sight I have ever seen. Her eyes are red from constant weeping. She looks like a very sick girl, but she insists that, if her father finds out, he will kill her. I don't see how she can hide indefinitely. He'll have to know sometime."

Everyone was talking now, and words were coming so

close together that it was hard for the girls to get the meaning of what was being said.

"Mrs. Lindgren saw her, too," said Lindgren. "She told me that at this point she looks like a haystack."

"What is wrong with looking like a haystack, Button?" whispered Karin.

"Poor girl," agreed Button, "imagine having a father that wants to kill you just because you look like a haystack!"

And as Button began pondering this situation of one so scared she had to hide from her own father, she was caught off guard, and the sneeze she had so successfully suppressed could be contained no longer. The noise from it came like an explosion, cutting the momentary stillness of the meeting room. She felt Karin's hand on her face, but it was too late. Deacon Lund opened the closet door and dragged out two shamefaced sinners to the surprise of the pastor and the other deacons.

"How did you happen to be in that closet?" he demanded angrily.

"We were playing a game about writing books," sobbed Karin. "We were going to get a story."

"I believe my daughter had something to do with this, too," said Papa.

Button avoided Papa's eyes. She wished the floor would open and swallow her up. Karin was sobbing wildly now, but Button felt no need of tears. She was thinking of Edith. At least she and Karin would not be killed because they had been discovered hiding.

"Did you hear all we said?" asked Deacon Lindgren.

"Never mind answering that," snapped Papa. "Can't you see the girls are nearly scared to death? I'm sure they were just playing a game. Button, you run on home to bed now. No coffee and cookies for you, young lady. And Lund, if I were you, I'd be lenient with Karin. I believe the girls have learned a good lesson and I'm sure they intended no harm but were merely playing a game not realizing that we had an important meeting."

Button did not tell Mama. She hurried to bed so she could be alone with her thoughts. The sorrow in her heart would not go away. It felt as if someone had placed a heavy stone there. She was sorry for kindhearted Mr. Anderson, who occasionally was tempted to drink, and even sorrier for Edith Strom, whose sin she did not know. She realized how fortunate she was to be a little girl with a good mama and papa. There seemed to be many things in life that were truly sad, and perhaps many people were weeping in darkness because they were frightened and lonely. If only she could help all these people. Perhaps someday she could, for she would write a happy book, one filled with joy and laughter. She might even write about a girl named Edith, but this girl would have a wealthy father who was good to her; she would fall in love with a wonderful young man; they would marry and live happily forever. But first she would begin by writing her thoughts in a diary, for then she could capture the mood of the minute. She would write down all the things she felt and not just the things she did, so her diary would be her very own and different from any other. And at the close of each page, she would write a brief letter to God. That was a beautiful idea! Instead of praying words to toss into empty air, she would write them in her book, and God could read them, lovely beautiful words that would never be lost, preserved for eternity!

It had been a terrible but eventful day, and perhaps all this would help her when she was ready to write her story. She knew that, after a night's sleep, she would lose her sadness and that tomorrow's sun would shine from the sky, warming her heart, but never again would she be tempted to listen in at a deacon meeting.

CHAPTER 3

ᴥ The Diary

In spite of her "special" talent, Button found it
was not easy to write a book. Three years had passed since
she had received her call, and in that space of time she had
filled hundreds of pages in her writing tablet with words,
but after reading what she had written, she knew that she
had not expressed what she felt and had torn out the pages.
Disappointed and frustrated after each writing experience,
she would run out to the garden or up the mountain slope
and find a faithful tree she could throw her arms around
while she cried her heart out. It wasn't really that the
words weren't good . . . she knew that if she showed them
to Karin, there would be great admiration in her friend's
eyes and Karin would think that Button had a great talent,
indeed. . . . But there was a discrepancy between the
words Button dreamed in her mind and the way they came
out on paper. The words on the paper weren't right; somehow they were not really Button's. Oh, some of them were
strange and pretty, but they were fake, as if she hadn't held
the pencil that jotted them down. It was not like her to give
up, however, so she tried over and over again in the hope

that someday she would be writing the words she felt in her heart.

She was thirteen years old when the miracle happened on a beautiful moonlit night. Button was leaning out the window of her room, drinking in the gentle beauty of the white summer night that surrounded the parsonage garden, when deep within her she felt something stirring and crying like the sound of music from a violin softly played. How glad she was that she was alone! She felt a wild desire to cry but did not know why, unless it was to ease the tension that had mounted within her and lodged itself like a big lump within her heart.

"I believe I can write tonight!" she whispered, stretching her arms toward the moon. "I am sure, Mr. Moon, that you will help me."

Going to her bureau drawer, Button took paper and pencil and sat very still for a few moments to enable herself to change from Button Franzon to Marry Terrier. She closed her eyes to blink back the stubborn tears. Then leaning over her paper, she began to write:

EDITH
by
Mary Terrier

The night was white with moonlight as a young girl named Edith walked alone along the lonely path beside a beautiful little lake. She had a rendezvous with a young man she had seen only once before. Harold was tall, dark and handsome but came from a very poor family, whereas Edith's father was a wealthy bank director. With Edith it was love at first sight as she recognized that this was the man of her dreams and even though he was poor in material possessions, he was rich in soul. Edith fervently hoped that the two of them were destined to dream many dreams together. . . .

Button wrote on and on and, as she wrote, the crying within her ceased and she began to feel light and gay. Her hand flew so swiftly over the pages she hardly had time to spell the words. The moon poured down its silver on her golden hair and the stars twinkled brightly and mysteriously in the dark night sky. It was exhilarating to be a writer, creating stories about people that existed only in her mind. When she read through the pages she had written, she knew that now, at last, the words she had felt so deeply had been transferred to the paper. It was the same sweet sorrowing sound of the violin, now playing a plaintive love song.

"I have actually started my very first book!" she cried jubilantly to herself. "I have really begun!"

Later that night, as she tenderly folded the written pages and placed them in her bureau drawer, she knew it to be the happiest moment of her life. Before she slipped into bed, she wrote in her diary:

Dear Diary,

Today I have started my book, EDITH, and someday I'll finish it. I know that it is going to be a delightful book and since you, my dear diary, are my closest friend, I shall share with you all the secrets of my heart. You will neither laugh at me when I do foolish things nor tell on me. I now in all secrecy confess to you that I am sorry that my Papa is a preacher. If he only could have been a doctor, or a lawyer, or even an ore-miner!

You see, because my Papa is in God's service, there are
a lot of things I can't do. I can't become an actress or a
dancer, and perhaps it is also a sin to become a circus
performer! Eternally I am supposed to keep in mind
what my Papa is and be a good example for others. I
am sick and tired of being good. I want to have FUN
and everything that is fun is sinful! What an awful
state to be in!

P.S.
Dear God,
      You know that I love my Papa very much. Please
forgive me for not wanting him to work for you. But,
why, God, have you made so many things that are forbidden? Can't you laugh at all? Why, then, did you
create laughter? When I behold the beauty of your sky,
I almost forget that you don't want me to have fun. Tonight your moon is particularly lovely and helped me
start my book. Thank you, God, for creating the moon.
Amen.

     One of the forbidden things that Button loved was to
watch young people dance. According to Papa's preaching,
dancing was a grievous sin. People who danced certainly
ended up in hell. Papa had used such strong words against
dancing that Button didn't dare to perform the steps her
feet were continually urging her to try. Sometimes the
temptation was so strong it was hard for her feet to remain
quiet, and then Button would inwardly rebel against Papa's
preaching and promise herself that she would learn to
dance as soon as someone would teach her. But when dark
night descended and Button was alone with her thoughts,
she would become frightened at having had such worldly

notions and on bended knees would promise God never again to think so sinfully. She humbly sought God's forgiveness, only later to lash out at the Almighty in her diary:

Dear God,

I can't understand it. The wind sways the trees in graceful rhythm and all the little buttercups dance in the sunshine. On the river the ripples shimmering in the moonlight look like a thousand "lille-put people" dancing. Why should a young girl have to feel like an ungraceful, clumsy and stiff lumber log, bobbing up and down in the stream, because it is a sin to sway your body and skip with your feet? If I am not supposed to dance, why did you put a desire and a longing in my heart to do so? Forgive me, God, for talking to you so frankly, but I am tired of thinking of you sitting up there in the sky pointing your long finger at me in condemnation and saying, "Look at her. There she goes now." You know I am unhappy when I do bad things and I admit I frequently do. Just now I feel like crying for ten years without stopping. Amen.

On a Saturday night when Button was almost fourteen years old, she took a long walk up the mountain road. Suddenly she stopped as she heard coming through the air beautiful music, laughter and singing. Button knew where it came from. There was a dance in Larson's red barn. Oh, how she longed to join those happy young people, but Papa had forbidden her to go near any such place. She hardly realized what was happening as her feet left the road and went hurrying across the field in the direction of the red barn. She walked as close to the scene of merry-

making as she dared and, finding a big tree, she stood behind it, making herself as small as possible lest she be
discovered. She need have had no fear, for everyone was
having too much fun to notice her. She embraced the tree
trunk, standing very, very still. A deep throbbing arose in
her heart, but she bravely fought the tears back. Look at
the good time everyone was having, so much fun, everyone
except her. A young couple who were dancing a waltz
caught her attention. As they danced, they were smiling into each other's eyes. They were the most beautiful young
couple Button had ever seen.

"Someday," she said aloud to herself and the tree,
"someday, I shall marry a boy that looks like that and he
will look at me as lovingly as this boy looks at his girl and
he will say, 'Darling, you are adorable, and sweet as a rosebud. As your petals unfold I want to be near to behold you
in all your beauty.' "

Still in a trance, she walked home slowly. The music,
the dancers, the moon, the warm summer night were almost more than she could take. She could not forget the
picture of the young man dancing. He couldn't be more
than eighteen and must either be a visitor or new in the
village, for she had never seen him before. She knew the
girl—Patron Lind's daughter. Those people never went
to Papa's church and right now Button didn't blame them,
for if they did, they never could have had the fun they were
having tonight. It was sinful not to go to church, but just
for tonight she would not let herself think of that. Instead
she would dream of that handsome boy who looked just like
the Harold of whom she had written in her book.

As Button sat down to write in her diary that night,

she pretended that she had come home from the party where she had been dancing with the new boy.

Dear Diary,
 Tonight I danced with my dream boy in Larson's red barn. He held me very close as if I were grown up. And do you know what? God wasn't mad at all. When I looked around, He had sent down four little angels who were dancing, too, in their little white robes. As I saw their radiant faces, I knew they were as happy as I.

P.S.
Dear God,
 Is making believe a sin? I hope not, for in my heart I feel that you are not cross with me. I see a lovely star that you tossed into the air millions of years ago when the world was new and without sin. It is winking at me. Please, please forgive me for having such a good time tonight. Amen.

It was fun doing things in her diary that she was not permitted to do in real life . . . almost as much fun as really doing them. When she fell asleep that night, she dreamed that she was grown up and that all the world was there for her to have fun in.

When Button reached her fourteenth birthday, she celebrated by having a party for her friends. Mama made a delicious cake and told her that she was almost an adult now, and Papa tickled her under the chin and said she was almost as pretty as Mama was when he first saw her. Button had grown very tall and slim, and she had a graceful way of walking that made her look more like sixteen than

her actual age. Her eyes possessed unusual depths for a girl
so young, and their color changed with the clothes she was
wearing or the mood she was in. Sometimes they looked as
angry as the turbulent river after a violent storm, but on
Sunday morning as she walked to church with the family,
her eyes were calm and blue as the summer sky.

At times during her fifteenth year Button became
very irate with her family, especially Mama. Button had
not altogether forgiven Mama for not having understood
about her "calling" and treating the matter so lightly.
Mama was the queen of her household and as the children
swarmed around her, like bees around their queen, Button
stood silently by, feeling strange and hollow inside, wanting to be close but hindered by an emotion that prevented a
feeling of oneness with them. It pained her when Mama
romped and laughed and sang with the other children. On
rainy evenings Mama would sit down on the floor of the
vardagsroom and gather her children in a circle around
her to tell them stories, but Button would withdraw from
the group, escaping to her room with the excuse of having
homework to do.

"I can never get that *apple-kaka* out of my mind,"
sighed Button when alone. "It was so much more important
than her own daughter that day long ago." She stood by
the window, watching the wind in all its fury whipping the
trees and flowers in the garden, bending them almost to
the ground. But tomorrow, when the sun shone, they would
rise again with a new beauty. Button lifted her head. Her
big eyes, staring into the darkness, looked almost green.
"If they don't break when they are bent low, neither will
I . . . never . . . never . . . " she promised herself "I
may have to bend, yes, at the blows of life, but no matter

how hard I am hit, I shall never break." She realized that the strength she possessed deep, deep within her, no one could take away. Nor could anyone pry into her thoughts or laugh at her imagination. She lived in a world of her own, a world within a world. She loved this new kingdom she had discovered, a place to which she could escape and be at peace from the turmoil surrounding her, a place of joy and laughter. These quiet times, the book she was writing and her diary were her closest companions.

Karin missed her gay company, for they did not see each other often, since they did not go to school together any more. But one afternoon they met accidentally and decided to go berrypicking along the ditches by the roadside. A little of the old closeness sprang up as they talked and laughed about schooldays. Then the mood changed and Karin complained as she faced Button, the *smulton*-berry-laden straw in her hand.

"What has happened to us, Button? You and I were the closest of friends, sharing everything, good or bad, and now we hardly know what to talk about."

"It isn't your fault, Karin," replied Button, trying to force a smile. "You see, I've discovered that I am different from other girls. Perhaps a writer is like that, wanting to be alone and acting as if she was crazy. I don't even get along with my own family. . . . I am different from all of them. . . . Sometimes I feel as if I don't belong in the parsonage—as if Mama and Papa were not my real parents."

"Perhaps you were adopted?" suggested Karin, trying to be of help. "Some children don't know they are adopted until the time of their marriage when it has to be revealed in the marriage papers. By then they don't care because they have a husband to love."

"How silly," laughed Button. "Why should my parents want to adopt a child when they have so many themselves?"

"Don't forget, Button, you were the second child—and —well—perhaps they wanted to be sure to have a girl after having had a boy."

This was a new idea to Button and one which gave food to thought. She worried about it as she went home to the parsonage, scanning the well-known surroundings in an unrealistic way. Perhaps this was the answer to why she was so different, so restless . . . and had been so naughty as a little girl. This would explain, too, why Mama was so impatient with her and why she hadn't taken an interest in her "calling." She studied her brothers and sisters and found they all resembled one another, but not one of them looked like her. The rest had a snug feeling of belonging and being wanted, whereas she was the odd, lonely one. Perhaps Karin was right after all. Papa hated red hair and Nim had been born with it. Perhaps Mama wanted to be sure that she would have a blonde baby and wasn't taking any chances. Somehow Button must learn the answer.

She thought she had done so when, on a Saturday afternoon after she had cleaned the parsonage kitchen, Mama came in to inspect her work. Usually Mama took it for granted that if Button had cleaned the kitchen it was clean, but not on this Saturday. She did something Button had never seen her do before. She ran a finger along the panels of the doors, frowning at the results. She opened the closet door, hung up an apron that was on the floor, placed a clean newspaper in the wastebasket, took a broom handle and poked under the sofa. Mama was rewarded for this effort by having toys of all descriptions come tumbling out as well as a soiled apron, a bib and even a stale crust of bread. Button was terribly ashamed, but her pride would not unseal her tight-closed lips as Mama's words showered down upon her.

"Button Franzon, I have never been so horrified in all my life! Just look at this mess! Do you call this cleaning? You know as well as I do that dirty clothes belong in the washbin in the hall closet and not under the sofa. And the toys! Since when have you decided that under the sofa is a better receptacle than the big box provided for them? I have a good mind to show Papa just what you have done. He'll switch you, big as you are! However, just this once, I am going to give you a second chance, but as a punishment you are to clean every bit of this kitchen over again. Even the parts that are clean you are to scrub, and it all must be accomplished before your bedtime." Mama gave Button a scorching look and marched out of the kitchen, her heels clicking.

Silent as she had been, Button was raging inside. It would be late when she finished, and her arms and back would ache from all that unnecessary scrubbing. Karin was right! There was no doubt now in Button's mind that she had been adopted. A real mama just wouldn't be so cruel to her own flesh and blood. Her eyes burned from having to hold back the tears so long and if she ever got to her room, she would let the flood loose. After that she would talk it over with her dear diary.

But later that night, when her work had been completed and she was once more in her room, the tears did not come for by that time her imagination was intrigued

by the wonderful story this would make. She had no time
for tears as she wrote in her diary:

Dear, dear Diary,
        You are still my best and very dearest friend and
I have shared many secrets with you. Now I know that
there is a great mystery concerning my birth. Karin
gave me the idea that I was adopted, but I believe
now that this is not quite true. Instead of being
adopted I am a changeling . . . even Mama doesn't know
this, but it explains why I am so much trouble and
why I love to go wandering at nighttime, forever
restless. I really belong to a gypsy family that visited
Lapland with their big wagon the year of my birth.
My Mama was a beautiful gypsy, hated by her mother-
in-law because she had wanted her son to marry
another. The night I was born and Mama in her weak-
ness slept, her mother-in-law stole me and ran to the
parsonage where a baby girl had just been born. In the
darkness of the night she exchanged me for the parsonage baby. I screamed and screamed because I wanted
my own Mama . . . that is why I am restless for there
is hot gypsy blood in my veins. Mama says she feels
sorry for my future husband, for I will not be a good
housekeeper, having a house that looks clean on the
outside but is filled with trash in places, like under the
sofa, where the casual observer does not look. She does
not realize how much work it is for a young girl to
clean a big kitchen and thinks I sweep things under the
sofa just for the fun of it!

Dear God,
        You are the only one that knows whether or not I
have written the truth. I hope that I am wrong, for I

don't really want to be a changeling. I do want more than anything else to feel that I really belong to someone, so if you don't give me an answer soon I may run off to join the gypsies. Amen.

Soon Button was faced with another worry. This time it was Papa. It struck her one night as suddenly as lightning will strike from a clear sky. During the evening meal it had seemed to Button that Papa had been too extra nice to her, passing the dishes of food to her twice and taking an interest in the little things, which was unusual for Papa, strictly out of character. Later he had sought her out alone and the words he had spoken had stunned her.

"Button dear, where did you ever get the feeling that you don't belong to our happy family? I hope it's a notion that will pass from you soon. All young people go through emotional conflicts before they adjust to being grown up, and you are no exception. Life is sometimes very hard for little girls who think they are big before their time. If ever you want to talk to your Papa about some of these problems, I'll be very happy to help you in any way I can."

"Thank you, Papa," said Button, "but I need no help. I am fine."

How could Papa so perfectly read her thoughts? She should have asked him, for a very disturbing thought was entering her mind, a thought she didn't dare to think. Where could Papa have received his information? Surely he who stood in the pulpit every Sunday morning and taught people how to live godly lives, surely he wouldn't go into her bedroom, open her third bureau drawer, look under her whole pile of underwear, and pull out her diary and read it . . . day after day, for how long? Oh, no, she just mustn't think such evil of Papa. The thought must have occurred to him because she looked so sad and never listened to Mama's stories any more. Yes, that must be it. But how could she be sure? She couldn't very well ask him! She would have to put him through a test that would determine once and for all whether or not he was guilty.

That night, when Button had finished writing in her diary, being very guarded about what she revealed, she placed a tiny white thread between the pages. This thread would be the determining factor in condemning or acquitting Papa.

For some unknown reason it seemed to Button that all the household went out of their way to be extra nice to her the next day. Nim gave her a picture of a movie actress he had cut out from an advertisement that had blown down. This was sweet of Nim as anything connected with the theatre was taboo in the parsonage. Nim knew how she admired those beautiful film stars. Pelle smiled his sunniest smile each time she passed him by, and Vickey asked her what apron she should choose for the next week of school, while Greta gave her the bigger part of the cookie she had received for going on an errand. Yes, everyone seemed to have been instructed to make her feel a part of the family. Even the little boys invited her to play a game with them, and Kerstin asked for help in tying her big red hair ribbon. What had happened? Had Papa told them about the talk he had had with his oldest daughter? There was no way of knowing, since she would not ask . . . not even if her life depended upon it. But it was so pleasant to be surrounded by love that she almost forgot about the adoption until Mama asked for her company on a short house call.

"It will only take a few minutes, and we'll have a nice walk home talking together," said Mama sweetly. "Somehow, Button, you and I seem to have grown apart!"

It was fun walking with Mama. All the old bitterness seemed to dissolve, and she even forgave Mama for not understanding about her being an author. Mama's sweetness was making up for it. They talked and laughed about many things that had happened at home or in the church.

"My," said Mama, placing her arm around Button's shoulders, "you are as tall as I am. And what a pretty girl you are! Please, dear, don't grow away from me. I want to be your very closest friend."

"Thank you, Mama. I know I'll need you. At times I do feel almost grown up, but there's still a lot of the little girl left."

"I hope that there'll always be a little girl for me to hug," smiled Mama, "and a big girl, too. How well I remember the day you were born, Button. You gave me the least pain of all the children, and you were the prettiest of all my babies, so tiny and delicate-looking except for those great big blue eyes. Even that first day they looked around as if to say, 'My, this is a funny old world I have come to live in!' And I hugged you to my heart. Believe me, Button, although I do have to scold you at times, you are still very precious to me."

Button laughed gaily, a big burden having rolled away. "I will not sweep things under the kitchen sofa again, Mama," she promised, mischief dancing in her eyes.

"I am glad, Button, for when you do things like that it reflects back on me, for I am the one who taught you to keep house. People who only keep a clean house on the surface are apt to be deceivers, hiding things in their own lives that they don't want others to discover. You see now why I was so cross finding you doing this very thing?"

"Oh, yes, Mama," answered Button mechanically, for she could hardly hear Mama's words above the tumult of her own feelings . . . her heart was singing with joy and the new happiness that filled her small frame was almost more than she could contain. Mama had proved by her words that she was not an adopted or exchanged baby at all. She was really Button Franzon and belonged to the family as much as any of the other children. How could she have had such foolish thoughts? Oh, to be alone in her room so that she could tell her diary the truth. Life was tremendously sweet and now she would go to work on her book and surprise them all.

When the supper dishes were done and put away and the kitchen as tidy as Mama would leave it, Button kissed Mama and Papa good night and hurried to her room. She was so excited that she took two steps at a time up the stairs. The door to her room was slightly open. She stepped inside and the smile left her face, her spirit sinking down almost to the tip of her toes. There on the rug lay the evidence, a tiny white thread. Papa was guilty! He had shared her every secret. She felt as if she were naked before a crowd of people and wanted to run and hide. Papa was reading her diary! Slowly she sank down on her bed, but the tears would not come. What a blessed relief it would be if she could cry, for now she felt all dead inside. Her new kingdom had been smashed to pieces. "I will never—never —never write in my diary again," she whispered. She pressed the book to her heart and then very slowly she tore out the pages one by one and threw them in the wastebasket. Then she crumbled the black cover. It had been so much fun to talk to her diary, but nothing that had fun in it seemed to last for her. There was still EDITH, the book. She rose from the bed and took it from the drawer. Tenderly she looked at it. Then she folded the manuscript and placed it in an envelope and sealed it.

"Never shall I finish it!" She spoke aloud. "Never, never, never! Edith shall never marry her lover. . . . Sometimes, when I am old and gray, I shall take it out and read it again, but tonight is the end of Mary Terrier. Perhaps I shall still be an author someday, but it won't be until I have moved from home and will have some privacy. Perhaps I shall never write, I don't know. I may be a complete failure."

Button knelt a long time by her bed. It was so much more difficult to speak to God than to write to him.

"Dear God," she uttered so softly that she could hardly hear her own voice. "You are all I have now. My kingdom has been lost, but please help me not to feel resentful with my Papa. I still love him so. Help me to understand and believe that you are my friend. Let me feel close to you, because right now I hardly want to live. I don't think I shall ever smile again. Amen."

When sleep finally came that night, Button had changed from girlhood to womanhood. She realized that childhood was past and that life was not easy to live when one was sad, but she closed her eyes with the thought: There is always a tomorrow, and the morrow could be better than the day before. She would not break . . . just bend—and this was surely bending very low.

CHAPTER 4

❧ Button and Beaus

Along the winding path up the mountainside young lovers walked arm in arm. Unspoken words of tenderness hung in the air. Down in the village the clock in the tower chimed nine times. As Button hurried up the path, she smiled to herself and there was mischief sparkling in her eyes. Here she was acting like an adult and she was only fourteen years and three months old! Yet romance had entered into her life and had completely filled every part of her being. Love had come in the form of Gunnar Borgeson, driving away the sorrow of having to give up her talent, a sorrow that had been so deep that she had been certain that all life's joys had come to an end. How wonderfully mistaken she had been! Papa, of course, knew nothing of this new stage she was approaching. If he had, Button was sure he would have unmercifully squashed it under his large foot as if it had been a bug come to plague the household. No, this secret she must guard as carefully as she would tread on sacred ground. She had tried to share some of her feelings with Mama, who had taken it for granted that the love she was asking about existed for Button only in storybooks.

"Are you reading books that Papa has censored, Button?" asked Mama. "You talk so strangely for one your age, and your eyes are full of dancing stars."

"Am I too young to ask about love?" returned Button. And seeing the laugh Mama was trying to suppress, Button decided to tell her nothing of Gunnar. But she would have to find a way to go on dates, and a way always opened for her when she desired something hard enough.

Button had found the way. Love, she thought, could come at any age, for there were certain things that slumbered in your soul until you yourself awakened them to life. Yes, she had found love bursting forth in full bloom the night she first met Gunnar.

"Of course, Papa must have forgotten how it felt to be young and romantic . . . it was so long ago," Button reasoned as she gazed at the round yellow moon, hanging low over the treetops.

What a divine feeling it was, this very first romance! But how would Papa feel if he knew about her and Gunnar? What a night this would be! Saturday night was made for lovers. All day long she had worked to help Mama ready the parsonage for Sunday. She had worked so hard and well that Mama had been really pleased, not knowing that Button only did it to make the time pass swiftly so nighttime would come sooner.

Now the lamps in the parsonage would be burning low. All would be still and peaceful. Button could picture it all in her mind. In the kitchen Mama would be finishing her last task of the day, that of shining the children's shoes. And in the study Papa would be going over his Sunday-morning sermon for the last time. He would be walking back and forth, sermon in hand, written in his big hand on lined yellow paper. Then he would stop, place the sermon on his desk and draw a circle around a certain sentence. That meant that at this point a good joke would be appropriate. Perhaps he would first tell it to Mama that night, for Mama was very critical of Papa's jokes. Button remembered hearing Mama tell him once:

"Pontus, your jokes must be so good that you yourself can laugh at them without effort. An ill-fitting joke will ruin the purpose of a perfectly good sermon. The people will remember the joke and not the gospel you are preaching to save their souls."

Papa believed in Mama's judgment, for in most things she was right.

Upstairs the children, with the exception of her oldest brother, Nim, would be in bed and asleep. But soon now Mama would be calling, "Good night, son! God protect and keep you!" And Nim would blow out his lamp and go to sleep. In her own room there would be a strange stillness. Button laughed, thinking of the form she had substituted for herself, which was now lying in her bed. It most certainly had the shape of a girl, and she had carefully pulled the quilt over most of the head. If Mama and Papa peeked in, they would never suspect that it was her dummy friend, Flora, reclining there, while their own daughter was scurrying up the mountain path.

Flora was a strange combination of a pillow, a cabbagehead and some hair from the roll Mama used to pin over her forehead when she was especially dressed up. Unbeknownst to Mama, Button had pulled a few strands a day and had then glued them to the cabbage. The blonde hair peeking out from under the bedclothes made a perfect disguise. Yes, Button had climbed into bed at the usual time but, instead of her nightie, she had been dressed in her Sunday dress and had to lie very still so as not to get it wrinkled. At eight thirty she had slipped from her bed, tucked her nightie under her arm, and laid Flora in her place. She had patted the hard head and whispered, "Be a good girl; don't you dare move and give me away," and she had pressed a quick kiss on the leafy cheek.

The front door had squeaked as she pushed it open, and for one fearful second she had held her breath. But Mama had been humming a hymn in the kitchen and Papa was reading aloud, so they had not noticed.

When Button was safely in the woodshed, she had hidden her nightie under a log and had flown free as a bird toward the mountain. To hide the nightie in the woodshed had been a brilliant idea, for if anyone awakened and saw her creeping into the house in her gown, nothing would be suspected as nocturnal trips sometimes had to be made to the outhouse.

Anyway, the happiness in Button's heart crowded out all fear of being discovered. For just a moment she had struggled with the thought that this might be a sin! Quickly she had dismissed this unwelcome idea, for even if it was, wasn't it worth sinning to meet Gunnar and be considered almost grown up? She tossed her pretty head and thought how silly it was of people to sleep away the beauty of the night. The wonderment of love, the gentleness and beauty of the night, the mystery of nature, stirred her so it almost hurt. Button had resolved to live life to its fullest, and no one would have the power to stop her. She would always seek until she found a way to fulfill herself. Right now, for instance, why should she sleep if she could be with Gunnar?

And then, through the shadows of the night, she saw him pass the bench by the lone pine and he was running to meet her. How handsome he looked with his green felt hat tipped back on his dark wavy hair. Although she couldn't see his eyes, Button knew that their dark brown depths sparkled with happiness. They clasped their hands and stood very still for a moment.

"You made it, Button!"

"Of course. Didn't you think I would? I promised you I would find a way!"

Their laughter echoed against the mountain as, arms entwined, they started to climb even higher. Gunnar held her tighter and whispered, "Sometimes, my little one, your bravery frightens me. What a child you are in years and still to me you seem as old as——"

"As you, Gunnar?" interrupted Button eagerly.

He looked down at the flushed face. "Yes, Button. You don't seem a day under eighteen to me."

"Good, then I won't have to feel that your going with me is as if you had robbed the cradle!"

He drew her closer and their steps sounded together as they climbed higher and higher in the stillness of the night. Presently they stopped and looked down at the village below them. Like twinkling stars that had lost their way, the small houses looked . . . stars lost from the sky.

Button placed her hand over Gunnar's mouth. "Let us not talk for a while, Gunnar, just stand here and be thankful that we can be together."

"Are you afraid our talking would break the enchantment, Button?"

"You mean all this happiness that makes us feel as we would burst?"

Gunnar nodded. They walked on in silence.

After a while Gunnar stopped.

"What if they should miss you, Button?" he asked anxiously.

She tossed her head indifferently. "Nothing much . . . a good thrashing and being forbidden to go out nights for a few weeks, perhaps. But nothing *can* happen! Nothing in the whole world! But even if it did, this night is worth it a thousand times."

They had stopped in front of a clump of trees.

"Oh, Gunnar, here it is!" Button held her breath. "I knew that sometime I would find it, just as in my dream. Can you see it?"

"See what, silly?"

"The house, Gunnar! *Our* house! If you dream with me, you will see it, too. See how peaceful it is in this spot so far away from the noise of the world and so near the sky. Our cottage is red and white and just big enough for you and me and our three children. I can see them pressing their noses against the windowpane, waiting for us. How beautiful they are—two boys and a girl!"

Gunnar laughed. "I am afraid your imagination is contagious, for I've been infected. I can see it, too, Button, through your eyes . . . and I like it. . . . It's fun seeing things that aren't there."

"It's called a second sight, Gunnar. I can always see things I want badly enough, and I can always make my dreams come true."

"I hope our house comes true!"

"It will, it will, Gunnar, if we dare to dream it long enough." Button took a step forward. "How low it is with the tall spruces standing watch over it. The two boys look just like their dad."

"And the little girl has a funny little nose like her mother's . . . and big blue eyes and golden curls . . . and when she smiles her teeth are as white as pearls."

"You have caught on, Gunnar; you're doing fine! Our curtains are real lace. We are rich, for you are the busiest doctor in town because everybody likes you . . . but I like you best of all."

"You crazy, precious girl . . . keep on talking like that."

"Our house looks homey, and see, there in the corner is your office with the sign on the door: GUNNAR G. BORGESON, M.D. You are so friendly to all the little children the mothers bring to you, bouncing them on your knee and putting your finger under the girls' chins, pulling their curls and telling them how pretty they are. And the old people come, too, for you listen sympathetically to their troubles and try to make them well again . . . only—oh, dear—it will take so long before you are a doctor and we can get married!"

"Perhaps we shouldn't wait. We could run away to Italy and by lying about our ages we could be married right away."

"Our happiness wouldn't last long in the loneliness of a strange land. Imagine Christmas when we would decorate our little spruce tree with roses, and I would be missing Mama and Papa and the rest of the family. I would soon grow sorry that I married you. I am always sorry when I do something wrong."

"I would kiss your loneliness away and call you my little dream girl!"

Button lifted wide eyes toward the star-studded sky. "Yes, it would be all right for you to kiss me then because we would be married."

Gunnar drew her close to his heart. "Button, may I kiss you now?" he whispered.

Button stared at him with unbelieving eyes. Then she laughed. "Of course not, silly! We aren't even engaged yet."

They ran down the mountainside. Strange sounds came from the woods, and the path was deserted. It was very late. Once on the parsonage road, they slowed their pace.

Button said good night to Gunnar outside the woodshed. "You must go quickly now," she whispered. "Papa might come out."

"Until next Saturday night then, precious. . . . I shall count the minutes."

She watched him walk away swiftly into the night. Then with haste she slipped out of her best clothes and placed them in a box she had behind the woodpile. Once in her nightie, she stepped out on the lawn to drink in again the mysterious beauty of the night that held so many promises of a joyful future to a young girl's heart. An eerie sound came from the mountain. Button shivered. The moon was high in the sky now. The stars were fading. Soon the sun would be lighting the eastern horizon. Alone up there on the mountain stood their dream house, unseen by human eyes.

Button breathed a prayer, eyes upraised:

"Please God, dear God, don't be angry with me tonight. Gunnar and I had such a good time. I love your beautiful world, but I love your nights best of all. Good night, Father God! I think I love you too, if you are not cross with me. Amen."

Late as it was, it still took Button a long time to fall asleep. Having put Flora safely away, her thoughts dwelt on the evening. If only she could share her feelings with her diary, but she just had to relive them in her mind instead. Once, she crept out of bed and knelt by the window sill still fascinated by the splendor of the night. So much she had wanted Gunnar to kiss her, but it would have been very, very wrong. The time would come when she would be old enough to act like other lovers, but at her age it would be a sin and God would be angry. Button felt happy knowing she had done the right thing and that even Papa would have been pleased had he known.

Back in bed again, she let her thoughts drift to the night she had first met Gunnar. If only she could have shared this experience with her diary . . . but her diary was no more. Thinking would be safer, since no one could read her thoughts; they would be all her own.

The meeting had happened the night she had discovered that Papa was reading her beloved diary. She had felt desolate, believing that never again would life hold any joys for her. After the parsonage had been stilled for the night, she had gone walking, as if that could relieve the terrible pain that kept mounting within her. She had taken the path that led to the lake, which was not too distant from the parsonage. It had been very early in the spring and patches of snow remained here and there in the shadows where the sun's rays had not yet reached them. The blowing wind had rippled the lake into small waves that made a soothing sound as they were tossed up on shore.

Suddenly Button's eyes had fallen on Gunnar, sitting on a rock not a stone's throw away. His head had been buried in his hands as if he were sorrowing, so she could not tell if he were young or old. She had stepped toward him and as he lifted his head she saw that he was quite young and very nice-looking and someone she had never seen before.

He seemed annoyed that someone had intruded upon his privacy. "Where did you come from?" he blurted out.

"Hi," answered Button. "I was just walking . . . but perhaps I'm not real . . . just a figment of your imagination, or a dream!"

"You could be, indeed." He relaxed. "There was no one here just a moment ago."

"I came like an angel to minister to your sadness or, if I won't do, you could try my Papa. He is the preacher in the village. But probably you are one of those people who never go to church."

"You are right. I don't go to church, and I don't need a preacher. In fact, I don't like them."

Button laughed. "At times I don't like them either."

"You are a strange girl." He laughed, too. "I came here to be alone in order to solve my problems and was angry with your interference, but I find that I like you and I'm glad you came. My father isn't a preacher, but there are times when I don't like him either."

Then he had told her his story. His father was the new director of the ore-mines and wanted his son to learn the business, but Gunnar had set his heart upon becoming a doctor.

"I hate the mines. It's like attending your own funeral to go down into the deep, dark ground with only a small light on your forehead. Each day I feel that I can't possibly descend another time, but my father refuses to listen to me. He says that at eighteen I'm not old enough to know my own mind!"

They talked at length that night and afterwards met whenever they could, and now each Saturday night there were the mountain walks. They both felt that they were deeply in love and though Button had told him she was only fourteen, to him it did not matter in the least, for she seemed so much older. She had told him that he must learn to dare to dream dreams.

"Gunnar, you must believe that you can be a doctor. You must dream it a long, long time, and then it will happen. Dreams are very much like stars——"

"Like stars? What do you mean?"

"Well, at times when you look up, the sky is bright with them, and then again you see no stars . . . but if you take the time to gaze long enough, you'll see that they're really there by the millions. Then you wonder why you didn't see them before. It's the same with becoming a doctor. You must see yourself with the black bag in your hand . . . and don't ever see the light on your forehead or the black pit again . . . blot them out from your mind. Gunnar, I can teach you to dream beautiful dreams!"

And she had, until now they were dreaming together, and tonight he had asked to kiss her. Button had wanted him to do so very, very much, more than anything in the whole wide world. But she couldn't spoil her happiness by sinning, for then the spell might be broken. "Oh, Gunnar," she whispered, "I love you even more than my diary!"

Slowly the picture of him faded from her mind . . . her eyes closed, the long lashes lying like half-moons on her flushed cheeks. Now and then they fluttered a little as if they objected to closing out the new day that peacefully embraced the parsonage in its gentle arms.

If Button could have seen Gunnar, she would have known that he, too, had tossed restlessly, thinking of her, of the night he had met her, of each meeting since, and wondering how life had ever existed without her. Yes, he was in love with a little girl of fourteen who was in both mind and body too mature for her years. What a strange combination this daughter of a preacher was! She could speak of love and marriage as easily as breathing but refused to be kissed. Her hand was warm and responsive and her eyes as bright as the stars of which she had spoken. She could actually make him believe that his dreams would come true. Already he was seeing himself as a great doctor, living in a cozy cottage up the mountain road with a beautiful wife and three lovely children. He could reach his goal with Button beside him. She was foolish and brave and with her sweetness drew him to her and then unmercifully pushed him away. His blood pounded in his veins at the thought of his lips pressed against hers. Like honey they would feel . . . fresh and pure. . . .

CHAPTER 5

❧ Tender Roots

Dummy Flora was no more! She had come to as inevitable an end as had everything else of value and importance in Button's young life. Almost like a funeral her going had been, with a stern preacher officiating, but minus the flowers and tears. For Button had not shed even one tear when she saw that her faithful friend had been shattered into her original elements—one cabbagehead, one pillow with a rope tied around its middle and a tuft of fine blonde hair.

Poor, poor Flora! She had been lying there innocently in Button's bed on her usual stint of Saturday-night duty when, without warning, the door had been pushed open and Papa had entered. . . . Now that it was over and Papa had left (How funny he had looked in his short nightshirt and bare feet!), Button was able to reconstruct what must have happened. A few minutes ago, Papa and she had had a long, long talk, for he had not spared the words. . . .

At nine o'clock last evening he had come to her room with very important news. Thinking she was asleep, he had tiptoed to her bed and remained there motionless for a few moments while he had decided whether or not he

70

should waken her. Button could picture him standing there, and then making up his mind, suddenly touching what he thought was a soft shoulder and bending low to whisper into what should have been a pink ear.

"Button," he had murmured, but all that greeted him was a strong whiff of wilted cabbage. It had not taken Papa long to discover that the smelly object substituting for his daughter actually was that—a cabbage! His unpredictable daughter must be out in the night, wandering about in her nightgown, gazing at the starlit sky. Yes, Button was sure that must have been what he had been thinking. He must also have conjectured that he was wrong in believing that Button had become a good girl. She was still a problem! There simply was no accounting for the strange things she did. My, but Papa must have been angry, for he had flung Flora from the bed with such force that she landed in the corner by the dresser, completely dismembered. After that he had calmed down a bit and crept into Flora's place under the gay patch-quilt to await his erring child's return. During the long wait Papa had napped now and then, and the brief snatches of sleep had served to better his mood somewhat, although he was deeply disturbed by the lateness of the hour. Then he had heard the unsuspecting Button creeping into the room. Her face had been flushed and her eyes dancing like stars after an enchanted night on the mountaintop with Gunnar. She had reached out her arms as if to embrace the whole world, and taken a couple of dancing steps toward the bed and jubilantly bent down to hug her friend.

"Flora, darling," she had whispered dreamingly, "You are an angel to take my place . . ." and as suddenly as a flow of water is stopped by turning off a faucet, her words

ceased. Flora felt so strange and soft. Presently Button
realized that, instead of a cabbagehead, she had grabbed a
human one fastened to her Papa, who was gasping for
breath.

Button blinked and stammered in surprise, grasping
for words that were not there. She felt like laughing and
crying, like shouting and whispering, while all the time
she was trying to think up an excuse that would save her
from this dire predicament. She stared into Papa's eyes,
penetrating eyes that pierced through her as they stared
back at her unmercifully.

Finally she spoke in a quavering, raspy voice, pre-
tending to be gay. "But, Papa, what in the world are *you*
doing in my bed—and at this time of the night?"

"What do you think I'm doing?" snapped Papa bitterly, his eyes shooting flames. "I've been waiting for hours
for you, young lady!"

Button made a great effort to look small and demure
as she stepped out of her slippers and crawled up on the
foot of the bed.

"I was wandering around, Papa. I wasn't at all sleepy,
and I felt a wild desire to go into the night. Why did God
make the nights so mysteriously lovely if we must sleep
them all away?"

Papa was caught off guard by this unexpected question, so he did not respond immediately. In the interval of
silence Button shook with fear, thinking that Papa was trying to figure out a punishment that would be great enough
for this, the latest of her crimes. After what seemed to be
an eternity of waiting Papa spoke:

"Button, I came here to talk to you. It was only nine
o'clock then." He paused for a moment. "Mama and I

will give you permission to wander, as you call it, out into the night whenever you like. You will have no need to use a dummy or any other invention you might dream up. Just let us know that you are going, bid us good night and for goodness' sake go out with your clothes on. Walk out through the door in a proper fashion, then there will be no law to break."

Button couldn't believe that she had heard Papa's words correctly. If she had, he must have lost his mind! Perhaps studying too hard for his sermons had made Papa sick. Was that why she had found him sleeping in her bed instead of being with Mama where be belonged? What other reason could there be for his giving her permission to run out in the night as she pleased, not even caring if she ever slept? Something was very, very wrong, for Papa was acting entirely out of character. Perhaps she had better run and fetch Mama and tell her that Papa was sick, indeed.

But Papa had sat up in bed, pushed the pillows against the wall and leaned against them as if his last words had taken all his strength. Then he spoke again, this time with a calm, preaching-a-sermon-at-prayer-meeting type voice:

"This evening Postmaster Olauson delivered a very important letter for which I had been waiting a long time. In six weeks we are moving to America. That is why I am granting you permission to roam around. Enjoy all of nature, night and day, in your dear homeland, for you will soon bid it farewell. I trust you will not misuse your freedom."

"Oh no, Papa," promised Button, too stunned to believe that what he was saying could be true.

"Button," said Papa more kindly, "I wanted you to be the first one to hear this news. It shouldn't surprise you too much, for you know Mama has talked America for years, and you also know that recently there has been a strong possibility that I would receive a call from over there. All you children wanted to go, so what could I do but acquiesce? Well, now the time has come, and the day and the hour will come fast."

Button swallowed hard. Papa didn't sound as if this was good news. He looked very sad. How thoughtful he had been to come and share the news with her first. She was sorry that again she had disappointed him. But how could she tell him that she had changed her mind about wanting to go? She couldn't tell him about Gunnar and risk losing the freedom just granted her. She must act happy despite the hurt in her heart.

"Perhaps we shall all like America," she said. "Perhaps Mama's dream of having us all educated will come true. Perhaps even you will like it, Papa."

"Leaving Lapland, Button, will be hard for us all. To pull up our roots from the homeland soil is not easy, and yours are very young and tender. It will be the hardest for you because you love your country with a true heart, but your roots will also transplant easier in the new soil. Don't worry about it, Button. Mama has the best in mind for all of us, and she is always very wise and right in most things."

How kind Papa was and how touching his concern for her. Papa had needed her tonight. He had felt that they belonged together in this parting. Her strong Papa had needed to be comforted! This was a new side of him that Button hadn't known existed. He was human and became bewildered and confused at times just like the rest of the family.

Her arms crept around his neck. "It will be all right,

Papa, and I thank you for the freedom to wander. I'll try hard to be a good girl."

She did not know how many times she had given him this promise, and she had always meant it. Perhaps this time she would keep it.

When Papa left, Button stretched out in bed. It had been a very eventful night, indeed.

Presently her door opened and Papa stuck his head inside.

"I just happened to think, Button," he whispered, putting his finger to his mouth, "that you better not tell Mama about the dummy. There are some things that are just as well for your Mama not to know."

"I promise, Papa. You and I alone will know about Flora."

Papa smiled happily, as the door closed, and a silvery string of laughter rolled from Button's lips. Quickly she covered her mouth with her pillow. It would be a sin to laugh aloud this time of the early Sabbath morning in the parsonage, but the scene with Flora had been so funny. Papa is afraid Mama will laugh at him, Button thought, but sharing a secret with Papa really made her feel close to him.

Although the night was mostly spent, it was hard to go to sleep. The time was so short before she would be moving away. What would America be like? When Button finally slept, she dreamed of houses so tall and straight they reached into the clouds, of wide stone streets where richly dressed people strolled, and of dollar bills raining from heaven.

When she awoke, she was in a happy, excited mood.

After all, if she did not like America, she could always return to Sweden, and Gunnar would be waiting for her . . .
Gunnar and their dream house up on the mountaintop.
She would not worry about the future because all the new
tomorrows could be better than all the yesterdays . . . she
could make them that way.

How fast those six weeks flew by and what a conglom-
eration of emotions they contained: excitement, anticipation, sorrow, joy. It was bitter-sweet, this leaving of
one's country, and it was hard to believe that the whole
thing was not just one fantastic dream. Every day there
were farewell parties and speeches, and gifts of every de-
scription poured into the parsonage. People were constantly coming and going, and Mama was as happy as a
young bride, singing and laughing the days away. Papa
tried bravely to look happy, but Button knew the sadness
that lurked beneath his smile and saw how heavy his steps
had become. Pulling up those roots is hard for him, she
thought tenderly as she watched him going down the path.
Papa did not like to move away! And her heart ached for
him. She had been unable to analyze her own feelings.
There was a numbness in her heart—or was she refusing to
face the issue? If she looked deep, deep within herself,
would her heart be crying?

Button was in a gay mood when she told Gunnar the
news. It was hard to see the light disappear from his eyes
as if she had struck him.

"Don't take it so hard, Gunnar," she begged, smiling
so her mouth hurt. "Just think of how many new things I
will see. Lapland here in Sweden is not such a big place,
after all. And you can come after me. You can get rich quick

in America, and then you will have all the money you need to study and be a great doctor. People over there have so much money they don't know what to do with it. Some of them throw it away just for a lark. Why, all you have to do is to stand on a street corner and a man driving a big automobile is liable to come up to you and say, 'Young man, you need this so you can take that pretty young girl for a ride. Will you do me the honor of accepting it as a gift?' What could you do but accept? And then I could smile my prettiest smile and say, 'Thank you kindly, sir.' Oh, Gunnar, can't you see how wonderful it all will be! And each summer we could come back to Lapland for our vacation. Please, please don't look so sad. If you like, I will give you my promise before I leave."

"You are still a crazy girl, Button," laughed Gunnar. "What in the world will I do without you! But, little one, I will not extract any promise from you. You are so young and bubbling over with life, everybody will love you."

Gunnar looked past Button as though he was trying to see the unknown years ahead, long empty years without this precious girl.

"I want you to be free, Button," he said slowly, "when you go out into that big, wide, unknown world. If you really love me, space cannot separate us, and you will come back to Lapland someday and we will marry here. But you may meet someone over there who will claim you and your love, so the greatest gift I can give to you is not to tie you down with words . . . only your heart shall belong to me until it makes its choice."

"Oh, Gunnar, Gunnar! You talk as beautiful as my Papa when he's preaching. I'll never forget you. Never, never! I shall give you a gift, too." Button hesitated a mo-

ment as though she was wording very carefully what she
was to say. "Gunnar, I shall give you Karin Lund, my best
friend, for a pal . . . only . . . just be friends. She is a
deacon's daughter, and she will talk you out of your blue
moods. Karin will be very good for you, Gunnar."

Gunnar smiled sadly. "Thank you, Button. I know you
mean well, so I'll be a good friend to Karin because of
you, but I assure you, we will be friends and nothing
more."

Something hurt deep within Button's heart as though
a needle was being pressed into her tender skin. Into her
mind had come the picture of Karin and Gunnar strolling
up the mountain path alone . . . and she—Button—
would be far, far away . . . and who could tell? . . .
Karin was so lovely that before long she and Gunnar could
be more than just friends. Perhaps it would be that Karin
would live in the dream house with Gunnar. . . . But,
then, there could be a new love waiting for Button, too.
Life was full of surprises.

That night, as Gunnar and Button stood on the mountain by their clump of trees, Button could no longer see
their dream house. It had completely disappeared from
her vision. She said nothing to Gunnar, for she knew the
secret of dreaming. If once you let a dream go, you can't
recapture it, no matter how hard you try. Even if you only
subtract a bit from its substance, it dissolves and is no more.
She tried not to be sad, for she had brought it on herself by
her gift of Karin to Gunnar, and now she must determine
to be happy because those two, having each other, would
be less lonely without her. Papa had said it would hurt to
pull up her roots but now one, at least, was pulled, and
though she would see Gunnar again, the agony of the pull-

ing would be over. However, there were two more to go: one for Karin, and the biggest and deepest of them all, the one for Sweden, her dear homeland.

Karin had taken the news very hard. Ever since that Sunday when Papa had read his resignation in church, she had followed Button around like a shadow, even spending most of her time in the parsonage.

They were sitting talking in the parsonage garden. Karin's enormous eyes never left Button for a moment.

"You're just born lucky, Button," she said in a high-pitched voice. "First you are going to become an author, and then you become the special friend of the handsomest boy in town, and now you are going to America where you are sure to marry a millionaire and won't have to lift even your little finger in work."

"Oh, Karin, don't talk so silly. If a millionaire comes along and wants to marry me, I'll simply say, 'No sir, don't marry me. Go over to Lapland and find my best friend. She is prettier than I!' "

They both laughed, sounding as though they were still schoolgirls together. There was so much to talk about, so much to remember. Button told Karin of her gift to Gunnar.

Karin blushed. "Oh, I can't ever fill your place, Button, but I'll do my best if it will make him less lonely for you."

"Thank you, Karin," said Button in a sad voice. Karin's eyes were as big as saucers and they sparkled with a strange gleam. Perhaps it had been foolish to ask Karin and Gunnar to be friends, but it was too late now.

The next night the two girls walked up to the little

red schoolhouse on the hill for the last time. They sat on the broad stone step reminiscing.

Karin took a small package from her pocket. "I brought you a little gift, Button."

"Why, Karin, how sweet!" Button admired the wrapping. "How pretty! Shall I open it now?"

Karin nodded her head vigorously.

Button took her time in undoing the ribbon. The box was white, the ribbon blue, and the paper red.

"I hope you notice that I chose the colors of the American flag," said Karin anxiously, "red, white and blue."

"Thank you, Karin. You think of everything." Button had tears in her eyes and Karin was sobbing aloud by now.

Then the box was open and Button stared at its contents, trying to hide her great disappointment. "I—don't know what it is, Karin. . . . It looks like garden dirt!"

"It is, Button . . . just plain, pure garden dirt, the greatest gift I could bring you. Someday, over there in your new country, you will be terribly lonesome for your old country and you can take a little dirt between your fingers and say, 'This is Sweden! I am home again!' "

"Oh, Karin. . . ." and they were in each other's arms clinging as if they could never part, "you think of the dearest things. I love the dirt and I'll always keep it, and each time I see it I'll think of you."

"And then someday give half of it to your minister— and when you die over there"—Karin was crying so hard she could hardly talk—"when they bury you in foreign soil —he can sprinkle some dirt from your homeland on your casket. . . . Oh, won't that be wonderful! . . . the soil of Sweden sprinkled on you—its own daughter."

"Please, Karin—don't. . . . You make me cry away

all my tears. . . . I—don't want to die—not until I get so old I can't walk—but it was sweet of you to think of my funeral."

"I don't want you to go, Button. Please stay here. . . ."

And Karin carried on so that Button was almost unable to control her. Never had she realized that she meant so much to Karin.

But later Button and Karin dried their tears and were happy again. It is hard to be sad for long when you are young and the excitement of life is before you. So they walked arm in arm down the road just like old times. But Button slept with Karin's gift under her pillow—a strange gift, indeed, but very precious. She would always treasure it.

On the last day in Lapland, Button was excused from all work.

"Let her go, Maria," Papa told Mama. "I will help with the children. Let her wander to her heart's content. This will be the last time, because the freedom of walking in the woods might never come again."

Mama laughed. "Pontus, you talk so strange. There will be mountains and woods over there, too, and lakes and flowers and song and laughter. You talk as if we were moving to a desert island."

And we might as well be moving to the desert, thought Button as the last farewells were being said. Alone, late at night, a gentle spring night that she would long remember, she strolled through the parsonage garden bidding each bush and tree good-bye. Removing her shoes and stockings, she padded across the soft green grass, reliving the thrill she used to get as a child at having the grass tickle her bare feet. It couldn't be possible that all the things in the garden would keep on growing after the Franzons moved away from here. In years to come, if they ever returned to this garden, all would look different, she reflected, as she took one last ride in the swing in the spruce tree, feeling as she had so many times before that it took her over the treetops and the blue mountains to the top of the world.

"I am not going to be sad." She talked to herself. "I must believe in my heart that in my new country I'll find trees and bushes and mountains and new friends." But her heart felt heavy within her, and the smile that she wanted to bring forth froze on her lips. In the stillness of the night she thought she heard a heart beating loud and hard way deep down in the dark dirt of the earth.

"It is the heart of my homeland," she said to the lilac bush, thinking sadly that it was budding and she would never see it bloom. "Mother Sweden is sorry when one of her daughters is about to desert her."

Suddenly she remembered what Papa had said about her roots being tender. He had forewarned her of the sadness she might feel when she took her farewell. She simply would not let herself be sad. She would force herself to feel gay and not to cry. Feeling the tears in her eyes, she started to sing a gay little folk tune to drive them away

> *"Jänta o ja*
> *Jänta o ja*
> *allt upp pa lantavägen o ja*
> *Jänta o ja*
> *Jänta o ja*
> *allt upp pa lantavägen. . . ."*

She sang it very softly so as not to awaken the rest of the inhabitants of the parsonage. She was lucky that Papa and Mama had let her be free to wander. They had been very good to her. Her heart was light again and her feet danced a little on the lawn. Then she picked up her shoes and stockings and, without another look at the garden, she ran up the steps to the parsonage.

Button had never imagined that the ocean could be so big. Gazing at it from the deck after four days at sea, she felt as if it had no beginning and no end, that it was only an endless span of water. Papa had said that in some places it was as deep as it was wide. This she could not fathom, the thought was so tremendous. Today Papa was standing beside her, the two of them alone, and he had thrown his arm across her shoulders. It felt safe and good to stand there with Papa.

"Isn't the ocean one of the most wonderful of God's creations! There's no end to it," exclaimed Button, trying to strike up a conversation that would accord with Papa's thinking.

"It is, indeed," smiled Papa. "I'm so happy that you notice things, Button, and that you respond to things in nature. Some people go through life with eyes which see not and with ears which hear not. This always makes a void, empty place within the soul."

"There are lots of people like that, Papa. You can almost single them out from a crowd. Their faces are always restless and unhappy-looking."

Papa's eyes scanned the mighty waters.

"The ocean to me is a true picture of life, and we are like the ship. To travel safely across the water we must have an able captain. Button, my girl, if you make God the captain of your ship, you will never have to fear the storms of life which are bound to come, and though you may be tossed about on the angry waves, you will be safe. Your ship may creak and groan, but it will never lose its course. And at times the ocean will be calm and gentle as a mother's love; it becomes like a mirror with the moon showering silver upon it and millions of stars glistening over it. But the ship sails on in sunshine and shadow, in storm or in calm, never losing sight of its destination, and our captain sees that we reach the goal."

"I'll treasure your words always, Papa. I like you to talk to me like that, especially now when we're moving to a new country and it may not be easy to be replanted."

They stood in silence while the wind blew the ocean spray in their faces. How far they were from Sweden now!

"Button, was it hard?" asked Papa tenderly. "Did it hurt to pull your roots from the homeland soil?"

She nodded, smiling up at him with bright tears in her eyes. He wiped them off with his big handkerchief. "There now," he soothed, "no use crying."

Button took a deep breath. "Last night I was homesick for Sweden, but it's all over now. I don't like to hurt very long. Will it also be painful to be replanted?"

"No," answered Papa. "There is no pain in that process, just loneliness. It will take patience, of course, but your roots will soon start growing again in the new land. You are young and strong. As for me, I was too old to pull up mine; perhaps they will wither and die."

As they watched the great waves rolling against the ship, they held on to the railing so as not to be knocked down by the wind. Here were father and daughter, so far separated by the years and yet so close in spirit. Perhaps the green-capped waves knew what the future would hold for these immigrants to a strange land?

Button patted Papa's hand. "Your roots will grow, Papa," she said sweetly. "God will see to that."

After Papa had left her to join Pelle and Nim for a walk around the deck, Button continued to stand by the rail, for she never tired of watching the waves or thinking upon the mystery of the sea. Her thoughts sped swiftly across the green water to Lapland, to the little white church, the dear parsonage, and to her wonderful friend, Karin, with whom she had shared so much of her life. And then Gunnar—dear, dear Gunnar, so fine and lonely—now left to dream his dreams alone, for no matter how sweet and funny Karin was, she did not know how to contrive dreams.

Button smiled as she remembered that last date with Gunnar when she had brought Karin along to introduce them to each other. At first Gunnar had looked surprised and disappointed, but Karin had been sweet and tactful.

"I know that two is company and three is a crowd," she laughed, showing even white teeth, "but Button insisted that I should come along." She put her finger against her short nose. "It won't be long though, just walk me home, and we can talk on the way. I wouldn't think of spoiling your last night together."

"Of course you are not spoiling our night, Karin. How silly! We're glad you are with us. Aren't we, Gunnar?"

Gunnar nodded his head.

"Gunnar, this is Karin, my very best friend. . . . Karin, this is Gunnar whom I hope you will soon know real well."

Karin smiled. There were deep dimples in her rosy

cheeks. Her eyes sparkled, and Button thought she had never seen them look so enormous. Karin was tiny and cute, and the smile never left her lips. She held out her hand to Gunnar.

"I know we will be good friends, Gunnar. I'm so glad to meet you. I hope you'll come to my house sometime and taste my Mama's cookies."

Gunnar laughed. "I'll never refuse an invitation to sample cookies. When may I come?"

"Oh, any night as soon as Button leaves."

"Now listen, you two," protested Button, already feeling left out, "it seems you can't get me off fast enough."

"Well, there's nothing we can do to stop you from leaving us, Button," said Gunnar lightly.

"I wish you wouldn't go, Button," sighed Karin. "You know that! But I am glad to meet Gunnar. . . . Gunnar, you are the most handsome boy around town."

Gunnar bowed deeply. "Thank you, Karin. Already I know we'll be good friends."

Button remembered how she wished Karin would not spread compliments quite so thickly. But that was Karin, always diving into things head-on.

"We'd better start walking," she had said, putting one arm in Gunnar's and the other in Karin's.

All the way to her house Karin had Gunnar laughing, and Button felt relieved when they finally left Karin on her doorstep.

"I'll see you before the train goes, Button," said Karin, "and you, Gunnar, whenever you come to call on me."

They had talked about Karin most of that night.

"You didn't tell me how pretty your little friend was,"

said Gunnar, "and she really has a wonderful personality, in a different way from anyone I know."

"Karin is wonderful, Gunnar. Perhaps you won't even miss me when you two get together."

He held her hand tightly.

"There's only one Button in the whole world!" he said, "You know, little one, that I'll never stop missing you, Karin or no Karin."

That had made her feel a little more at ease, but as they were about to part that night she had impulsively given him her lips.

"You may kiss me, Gunnar," she had whispered, surprised and embarrassed by her own boldness. "I know we're not engaged, but I don't think a farewell kiss would be wrong when I'm going so far away."

Gunnar had stared at her, then his lips had touched hers for a mystic moment.

"Thanks, Button," he said in a husky voice, "thanks a lot. I'll never forget you, never."

He was gone and she had stood on the lawn for a while shivering a little inside. She did not know if she had committed a sin or not. God might be very angry with her, and Papa would be furious if he knew, but she had had to do something so Gunnar would never forget her. It was all Karin's fault, she thought. She had made Gunnar think she was very special. . . .

As Button stood there on the ship's deck she wondered if, before God, she was really engaged now. She didn't know if that would make her happy, because already Gunnar seemed far away and perhaps in the new land she might meet someone even more wonderful than Gunnar . . . perhaps. . . .

"Good evening to you, young lady," said a masculine voice behind her.

Button turned quickly and faced a young ship's officer, tall and dark, with a winning smile.

"Oh, you frightened me so I could have dropped right into the deep blue ocean," laughed Button, "but good evening to you anyway. It's a very lovely evening!"

"What's lovely about this one?" he teased, stepping beside her.

"The wind!" exclaimed Button, looking far across the sea. "The wind that blows greetings and memories from Sweden."

"You are homesick already?"

She nodded.

"I'm sorry that I'm part of the crew of this ship where we are forbidden to mingle with the passengers. If I were free, I assure you it would be a privilege to help you get rid of your loneliness!"

Button's eyes twinkled. "Already I've lost a bit of it!"

"What can I do for you?" he asked eagerly.

"Take a greeting back to my homeland."

"What shall I say?"

"Say that Button is doing fine and that she will dream a certain dream to a finish."

"I'll be glad to carry that message. You're an unusual girl and that's an unusual message. I like you, but talking to you longer might cost me my job . . . though perhaps it would be worth it. Good night, Miss Dreamer." He touched two fingers to his cap and, bowing lightly, walked away, straight and tall, without a backward glance.

Later, as Button entered her cabin, she could hear from the happy uproar that her family was waiting for her.

"There's something in your bunk, just for you, Button," cried her sister Greta, rubbing her hands in excitement. "And nobody knows who brought it!"

Papa looked very stern, but Mama was smiling, and everyone watched as Button pulled back the curtain . . . and there it stood—a large basket of the most delicious-looking fruit. Her eyes almost popped from their sockets. She found the note and stuck it in her pocket.

After the fruit had been divided and everyone had left happy, she read the note:

> See what the wind blew in! And
> all of it for the girl who likes to dream.

She slept with the note under her pillow and dreamed of the young man who had sent it. Only in her dream she was not sleeping on a hard bunk, but in a bed made of beautiful thorn-free roses. In the morning she woke up with a smile, and her heart felt light and gay. It was as though her roots were being planted before she reached the new shore, and all because a good-looking young officer had smiled at her and evidently thought her older than her years. Perhaps she would see him again? For after all, he had left her a most delightful gift.

CHAPTER 6

❧ Mama's Way

This is America!" said Papa one morning about three weeks after they had moved into the parsonage in Berkley Hills. "It is called the land of opportunity, but before we find out what it will give to us, we must learn to speak English."

"You and Mama can talk good already," said Pelle.

"Not well enough, my boy. We can speak enough to make ourselves understood, and the only way we can learn is by trying."

Button had never seen Papa in such a gay mood, but then the whole family had entered the United States with hearts beating with excitement and Papa, like the rest, was engulfed in the newness that was all about them. For days now the members of the household had shuffled furniture around and moved drapes and curtains. The parsonage had been partly furnished with pieces of furniture from the church members' attics, discarded things which they had thought would help the pastor's family until they could pick out what was needed. It had been a gracious, kind deed, and Papa and Mama had both been very grateful.

"Button," said Papa, "how about trying your first lesson in English this morning? I want you to take Vickey and go downtown and buy her a new dress. What color do you want, Vickey?"

"Blue," smiled Vickey happily. "Heavenly blue like the sky! But how can Button buy me a dress when she can't speak English?"

"That's the best way to learn, dear, by trying to make yourself understood."

"We can take the Swedish-American dictionary along," suggested Button, sliding the little book into her purse.

"Here," said Papa, "take this," and he handed Button a five-dollar bill. "You do a good job, now. You know I promised Vickey she would get a new dress when we came to our new country. Remember?"

"Perhaps I should go along," said Mama, looking a bit anxious.

"No, Maria, you would do all the talking. Let the girls try for themselves."

Mama walked with them to the bus at the corner, giving all sorts of advice. She handed them a piece of paper on which was written the place where the driver should deposit them.

Tremblingly the girls boarded the bus. They waved at Mama and sat very close together. This was a tremendous experience. What would happen?

Vickey looked up at Button with wide, fearful eyes. "Do you think you can do it, Button?" she asked in a low voice. "I'd love a new dress, but how can we buy it when you can't speak the language and don't even understand what is said to you?"

"I'll find a way," laughed Button. "I'll talk with my

hands." She opened her dictionary to the letter K, looking for the Swedish word, *klädning*, meaning dress in English. "Dress," she whispered to Vickey, "remember that word because we shall need it. Papa is challenging me . . . he doesn't think I can do it . . . but I will buy a dress . . . You wait and see."

Button and Vickey stood in front of the dress rack in Landen's Department Store. A saleslady came smilingly toward them, rattling off a long stream of words which made Button feel very stupid.

"Dress," said Button slowly to the salesclerk, pointing to Vickey. "Hurry," she said to her sister, "find *blå* in the dictionary."

Vickey put her finger on the letter B, and turned the pages. Button smiled her prettiest at the lady, showing her the money. The clerk spoke more slowly now, but it meant nothing to the girls.

"I can't find that word," sighed Vickey sorrowfully.

"Never mind," soothed Button. "See there on one of the dummies is a blue dress."

"Dress, dress," repeated Button, pointing to the dummy.

A light seemed to dawn in the clerk's eyes. She undressed the dummy and held the dress in front of Button. She asked a question. Button nodded, hoping it was the right answer. The lady smiled and ushered Button into the dressing room. She helped Button remove her own dress and slipped the soft blue one over her shoulders. Button tried to protest, but to no avail. A moment later she stood in front of a three-way mirror and gasped as she looked at herself in the glass. Could this beautiful elf be Button

Franzon? The dress was a dream, and the prettiest Button had ever seen.

Vickey's eyes were wide with wonder. "Oh, Button, you are simply beautiful! Just—just like a real princess! You must have that dress. It looks as if it were made for you. I'll wait awhile . . . but you must take the money and buy it . . . please, Button, do."

"But Papa! What would he say, Vickey? It is you who need the dress—but—but it's so beautiful!"

"Just buy it, Button. If Papa saw you now, he couldn't resist buying it for you. . . . We'll make him understand."

Button made no further attempt to make the saleslady understand. She paid for the dress with a trembling heart, and she and Vickey walked from the store carrying a big box between them.

"Are you scared, Button?" asked Vickey.

"Of course not," said Button. "It's done now! If necessary, I'll work and earn the money to pay for it myself."

They walked on to the bus in silence.

Both Mama and Papa met them on the parsonage steps.

"You really did it, Button! You bought the dress for Vickey!" cried Papa happily.

Button avoided Papa's eyes. "Almost," she answered.

"But you have the dress in the box," ventured Mama.

"But not for Vickey. . . . Oh, Papa, Papa! I got the darlingest, sweetest, bluest dress you've ever seen . . . but it's for myself. The lady could not understand that I wanted one for Vickey—and—and—I'll get a job and work for it. . . . I'll pay every penny of it. . . . Please don't be cross with me."

Papa smiled. He winked at Mama.

"Well, Button, I guess you tried your best even if the evidence is against you. Poor Vickey! As usual she gave in to make someone else happy. Mama and I will forgive you this time, and next week we'll take Vickey downtown ourselves, you can be sure, and that little girl shall have a blue dress, too."

Button smiled happily. She put on her new dress for the whole family to see and admire. It was a great day and America was a wonderful country. She just wished that Karin could see her now.

There was a freedom in America not present in Sweden. People walked with ease as if they needed not to take thought for the morrow, and they all laughed and played as if life was a wonderful playground and not a place in which to prepare for old age or eternity. It was fun living in this great big land, and little by little the memories of Sweden faded until it was hard for Button's mind to picture the old familiar places.

Of course succeeding weeks and months brought occasional times of adjustment to all of them, with many a wistful backward look to the peaceful days left behind in Lapland. However, the months and the years moved on as swiftly as a weaver's shuttle. When three years had passed since the Reverend Franzon and his family had landed in America, all of them seemed happy and contented in the new surroundings, though Button often wondered about Papa. Tenderly she watched him trying to embrace all the newness, but she feared that he still longed for his homeland and that he would never really take root in this new land. Although he never uttered one complaint, she noticed that his hair was almost white now and often there was a sad, longing look in his blue eyes.

Button was sure it was this feeling of restlessness that had caused Papa to ask his church for a leave of absence and to purchase a small farm out in the country by a lovely lake. He told the church board that he needed a rest for his tired mind and, kind as they were, they let him go when he gave his promise that he would return in a year or two if they still wanted him.

The farm was a new experience for them all, and Button found she had time to dream again. Anew and more urgently than ever the old call came as it had in the little red schoolhouse when she was a very young girl, the call that had lifted her to the highest pinnacle of joy and then thrown her down into the blackness of her own confusion. Now it knocked at her heart's door and begged to be recognized. She had done a bit of writing, a short story and a small volume of poems, but had not started a book. How could she write in a strange country? How could she express her thoughts in an unfamiliar tongue?

Thinking back upon the years that had gone by, there was much for which to be thankful. Button had learned many a lesson the hard way. She understood now that friendship, no matter how deep, and love, no matter how sincere, can burn out for lack of fuel to sustain them.

In the beginning, full of anticipation, she had awaited each letter from Gunnar and Karin. This was her tie between the new and the old world, and every letter had been full of love and longing. But as the time went

by the intervals between letters became longer and
longer, and the letters themselves alarmingly shorter until
they contained nothing but a record of the good times her
friends were having together. She had been hurt when
Gunnar wrote about the weekend trip he and Karin had
taken to go mountain climbing on Kebnekaise, especially
since he had elaborated on how much fun it had been.
Then came a letter in which he told Button he had given
up his dreams of becoming a doctor.

> Button [he wrote] I believe that my father may
> have been right the whole time. Now that I am an ex-
> ecutive in his office with a fine future ahead of me, the
> light on the forehead and the dark pit are only un-
> pleasant memories. They will never influence my life
> again. Thank you for helping me to dream that noble
> dream of someday becoming a doctor. I have given
> that dream up, but it was fun dreaming it with you. . . .

It angered Button to think that Gunnar could let go
of his dream so easily. But she did not let it trouble her for
long, for he was too far away to affect her life and each
day he seemed to get farther and farther away now that
they could no longer dream together.

Then one day Button received from him a thick,
heavy letter. She took it out to the garden, holding it in her
hand a long time before she opened it, for her heart sensed
its contents and she wanted to brace herself against being
hurt. And, of course, she was right. Gunnar had fallen in
love with Karin Lund, and he planned to marry her in the
near future. He thanked Button with all his heart for the
years that had been, calling them beautiful and sweet, but
most of all he thanked her for the gift of Karin.

I know [he wrote] that this is not causing you
pain or sorrow. When you left, I knew our dreams were
over, but I doubted that anyone could ever fill your
place. Karin did! She is adorable and likes to spring
surprises on me as you did . . . but in a different way.
I am sure you don't love me as much as she does and
that you would be most unhappy to leave America and
settle down in this godforsaken corner of the world. . . .

If she had imagined that this news would hurt, she
had been mistaken. Her love for Gunnar was gone. It had
either worn out or just faded away, and she was glad that
it would be Karin and Gunnar who would find happiness
in each other.

Karin was more concerned about Button in her letter
and fear crept between the lines as she wrote:

Button dear, if for some reason, you still have any
feeling for Gunnar, let me know. I will walk out of his
life faster than a lamb can shake its tail, if you ask me.
I am afraid that our being always together led to this.
We both know that, if you had remained in Lapland,
it would never have happened. Although I miss you,
I can't help blessing the day you left for America. I
will be honest, Button, these years with Gunnar have
been the most precious gift I could ever have received. . . .

Button crumpled the letter in her hand and tossed it
into the wastebasket. She lifted her head nonchalantly.

"And all she gave me was some dirt for my funeral,"
she smiled. And she sat down and wrote her friend a reas-
suring letter, wishing her happiness and telling her that

"after all, Gunnar had just been a passing fancy of youth."
She also wrote Gunnar a letter sparkling with fun. It
would be her very last letter to him.

> You know, Gunnar, life has a way of straightening
> us all out. I am glad that you never followed me to
> America for I have discovered that they don't give
> away expensive autos on street corners and that people
> really have to work to get their dollars. . . . I am glad
> for you and Karin! Love her a lot! She is a darling
> and dear as can be. . . .

So that part of her life was over. It left an empty
space in her heart for a while, but a date with a handsome
young man soon filled it. It was hard, however, to find a
young man that measured up to Gunnar, hard to find one
that measured up to her own ideals. Perhaps she never
would? She had been admired by more boys than many
a girl in her community, and by the time she was eighteen
she had had two proposals, but she had no wish to settle
down. Maybe she would be true to her calling and marry
her dream?

Button had had great difficulty in learning the new
language. Now she could laugh over it, but it had not been
so funny when she had made embarrassing mistakes because she did not understand. The only way was to laugh
at a mistake and learn a lesson from each one. All the rest
of the children had progressed well in speaking English,
but they had continued in school in the new land. There
had been quite a session that day in the parsonage when
Button had defied both Papa and Mama.

"I don't care how important it is to get a good basic
foundation in the new language. I shall not keep on study-

ing. Never! Never! I'm through forever with teachers. I
think you are both cruel even to suggest it."

Mama was very provoked.

"There is no shame in learning at any age and it
doesn't matter how old you are when you learn a language," she stormed. "You, Button, are a very stubborn
and foolish girl."

Button yielded not an inch when Papa put his foot
down and said that education was a necessity for *all* his
children. She was determined to win this battle and to
show Papa that, when it came to principles concerning
her own life, she could be as strong and unbending as he
was. She was made of the same stuff!

"All I'm going to do of importance," she said, tossing
her head, "is to write a book, and I certainly don't need
years in school to do that."

Button tried to ignore the pleading in Papa's eyes, but
it softened her a little.

"Don't worry about me, Papa," she laughed. "When I
write my book, words will pour from me like sugar from a
bag. I am going to write humorous things that will make
people laugh, you see; not textbooks."

Papa and Mama said no more. They knew they would
get nowhere with Button, for it was impossible to talk
sense to her. Someday she would pay the price for having
refused an education. Papa found Button a job doing
housework for an American family where nothing but
English could be spoken. He was very upset at his oldest
daughter's behavior and decided she would have to learn
the hard way. But now those years had gone by and Button spoke English quite well, and she was back with her
family on this lovely farm. Several times she tried to start

her book, but no words would come. Perhaps she had
boasted too much when she had said that writing would
pour out from her effortlessly. She had spoken out of ig-
norance, using words that had no meaning.

Button sat by the blue water of the lake below the
farm. The lonely, driving restlessness of her spirit had
prompted her to leave the family group gathered around
the organ to sing their evening hymn. When the long days
had ended, and the chores had been done, Papa again
looked like the preacher he had been for so many years.
Button had stayed until the prayers had been said and a
chapter read from the big family Bible that had been so
carefully packed and lovingly carried from Sweden. A
lump had formed in her throat and a wild knocking on her
heart had made her want to cry or run out and throw her
arms around a faithful old tree as she had done when she
was a little girl.

Perhaps I miss Gunnar, after all, she thought. Perhaps
I don't want him to marry Karin.

The music from the song floated over the water.
There was something so homey about a family singing together around the organ, the voices from the youngest to
the oldest mingling in harmony. If only that wild desire to
cry had not come, she could have been there, too! It always thrilled her to see Papa seated at the organ, his gray
locks curling around his ears and forming a curl in the
nape of his neck when his hair was as long as it now was.
And Mama's face always beamed as she sang, her eyes
twinkled like stars, and the smile on her lips was like a
heavenly benediction over those she loved. Nim would
lean hard on the organ and Pelle always stood close to

him. Vickey and Greta shared the same hymnal, their
faces intent and serious-looking. Calle and Torkel, the
other two boys, would have their arms around each other's
shoulders and little Kerstin, her eyes big and blue as blue-
berries, would nestle close to Mama. What a group they
made! . . . It was only Button who was missing, and if
they had noticed her absence by now, they would think
nothing of it, for wasn't Button like that—unpredictable,
always running off at the strangest times? One moment
her voice would ring with laughter and the next she
would be crying. Why? No one knew. She would be sweet
and cross to suit her fancy, so they all had stopped trying
to understand her. Well, how could she expect her family
to understand her when she couldn't even understand herself?

The gentle beauty of the night brought tears to Button's eyes and a longing crept into her heart. It was a longing for Lapland—for the mountain road—for Gunnar running to meet her, as he had so long ago, his brown eyes
sparkling with happiness. She longed to hear Karin's silvery laughter and to hear the bells chime in Papa's little
church on a Sabbath as the white summer night spread its
wide wings over her homeland.

Perhaps, coming to America had been a mistake!
Could it be that dreams remained in the land that brought
them forth and that she never would be able to write her
book in a strange land?

Button longed most of all for her diary! If she only
could forget the tragedy of the first one, she might start
another.

Then in the midst of her thoughts there seemed to
come a voice from within that spoke to her." "Button," it

whispered, "you're doing all right. When tomorrow comes you will smile again."

Over the waters was reflected the flame-tinted sunset sky. She raised her eyes heavenward. What a strange combination of clouds! Surely no artist's brush could capture their wild beauty. And up there in the clouds there was a door, partly open, right into God's heaven! A smile played on her lips, as she was thinking: Mama would say that a soul had just entered heaven and God had not had time to close the door. Mama said such strange things. She had such a childlike belief in the unseen. She literally talked to God, and He always answered her in a voiceless voice—at least so she claimed.

Button's head fell into her hands. She remained sitting in that position for a long while as she reached deep, deep down into her soul to try to find the great answer that she knew must be found somewhere. How did Mama get her answers from God? God did not speak in a human voice. Or did He?

Gently a hand touched Button's shoulder.

"Button"—came Papa's voice out of the night—"I wish you wouldn't follow your impulses and run away. This is the first time it's happened during our family worship. I don't like it at all, and believe me, my dear, you are the loser."

Button didn't mind Papa's mild scolding. Her heart beat fast with joy. Papa had missed her and had come to find her. Just to have him beside her took that awful loneliness away. She would talk to Papa. She would ask him things. Papa must know all about Mama and God.

She sat up and faced him as he seated himself on the large stone beside her.

"Papa, I am sorry. I don't know why I run away like that. There—there is something inside me that seems bigger than I. . . . It drives me and makes we want to run off. But I'm glad you came to me, very glad."

Papa placed his hand on hers, and they sat in silence for a while. Button was first to break it.

"Tell me," she said, "about Mama. How can she talk to God? I have heard her say words into the air as if God was a real person, walking and standing right beside her. And she seems to get an answer, Papa. She just waits until she knows God has answered."

"Mama has always done things in a unique way, Button. If I were you, I'd concentrate on being myself and not on trying to imitate Mama. Her talking is really praying. She just does it in an easy way, as naturally as breathing."

"If I did that, my voice wouldn't carry a prayer. It would just find its way over the lake and be lost . . . lost in nothingness."

"Button," said Papa in a kind voice, "God does speak to men. He always has and He always will. In the Old Testament He spoke to Moses in a burning bush and to Elijah in a still, small inner voice; and later in the Bible, to Paul, in a great shining light. All these men claimed that they heard a voice speaking, but others beside them heard none. God spoke, and they heard His voice in their souls. If you, dear, have something special on your heart to talk to God about, just talk to Him as you talk to me, and I know that when the answer comes you'll understand it. It is God's voice within your soul."

Papa stood up.

"I'll leave you now, leave you by yourself with your God. If you need me, I'll be in my study."

Papa placed a light kiss on her cheek and walked up the hill toward the house. Button walked along the road by the lake toward the woodland. She walked slowly.

Would she know the answer as Papa had said she would if she also prayed the way Mama did? Would God really answer if she prayed without kneeling and with her eyes open?

"Dear Father God," she heard herself say. "You know all the things I'm thinking and even the things I have hidden carefully deep down in my heart. Long ago, when I was a little girl, I had a dream of becoming an author and writing a book that would make people laugh and be happy. Please, God, make my dream come true. Help me to become a writer, God, please, please."

The night was quiet around her and slowly that tranquil stillness of peace floated into her soul. Her heart did not beat wildly as before. And so thoughts came to her mind—wonderful, beautiful thoughts that had not been there a moment ago. They came clear and fast . . . as fast as she could grasp them and she put them into words, speaking them slowly and softly as she walked along.

"I will write a book someday. Nothing will stop me now because God will help me. I shall dream my dream so high and it will be so lofty that it will reach a golden hill where God will keep it until I am ready to have it returned to me. I will eat it . . . I will sleep with it. . . . it will be so much a part of me that someday it will be fulfilled. God will fulfill it through me. . . . Thank you . . . thank you . . . for answering my prayer. My dream is like a delicate flower which will blossom and give me joy . . . in God's fullness of time."

Button's feet had wings as they flew back to the farm-

house. She began remembering the times she had heard
Mama talk to God, and now she understood it. She had
been very small the first time she had heard it. Mama had
gone upstairs to make the beds and Button was playing in
the big kitchen, in the Lapland parsonage. She knew
Mama was alone upstairs and yet she heard her speaking
as though someone was with her. Perhaps, she thought,
Mama is talking to me. She ran to the foot of the stairs
and called, "Mama, did you talk to me?"

And Button could still remember how surprised
Mama had looked as she came to the landing and looked
down at her with that warm smile on her lips, saying, "No,
little one. I didn't talk to you. I was talking with God."

Yes, she had wondered then how Mama did it, for she
was so strict when her children prayed. They had to kneel
and close their eyes and approach God in holiness and
reverence. And here Mama herself had been walking
around making beds, so she couldn't even have closed her
eyes. Button could not understand it.

Once Mama had been standing alone out on the lawn
gazing upward while a fine rain came down on her blonde
hair. But Mama did not seem conscious of the rain; her
whole face was beaming as Button heard her say, "God"—
and Mama had raised her voice a little as if it took more
volume to penetrate the clouds—"You saw the lawn
needed water. Thank you for sending the rain to do my
watering for me as I was much too busy baking. A great
big thank you, God."

She had heard Mama ask God to bless the dough
when she made bread, bless it so the yield would be large
enough to feed so many mouths; and she had asked Him
to keep the milk from souring in the hot summertime.

"Father God, You know that my children don't like sour milk, but if it does sour, You know they would have to drink it, because we can't afford to waste it."

Once, while Mama was holding Pelle's shoes in her hands, Button had overheard her talking to God as if she were scolding Him. "God, you forgot to answer my prayer of last week concerning Pelle's shoes. They are wearing out much too fast. Now I am asking You again, bless his shoes; he has such busy feet."

Button remembered all these things, but she also remembered that Mama believed in her prayers with a childlike simple faith. Never would she forget the school morning she had awakened with a sore throat and her body wet with perspiration. She tried to swallow but felt as if her throat was full of mashed potatoes mixed with gravel. She had sent Greta to fetch Mama so Mama could see she was in no condition to go to school. And Mama had come and placed her cool hand on Button's hot forehead.

"You are real sick, Button *lilla*," said Mama, "poor girl."

Button was thankful for Mama's sympathetic words.

"I am too sick to go to school, Mama, and we're having a very important lesson. Now the teacher will never know how well I learned it."

Mama asked all about her sickness. She shook her head as she looked at Button's throat.

"Yes, you have a good dose of whatever it is, but we'll take care of it. You believe that God does not want little girls to be sick, don't you?"

Button nodded. God cared about everybody. Papa said so. Mama placed her hand on Button's forehead and knelt down by the bed. Her prayer came hurriedly as if she did not have too much time to spare on a busy morning with seven children to feed and most of them to get ready for school.

"Dear God," she prayed, "You see little Button here in bed, too sick to go to school where she has an important lesson. I think she has a little fever and a sore throat, but those things are nothing for You, God, so I ask You please to make her well immediately. Thank you for being so good to us. Amen."

Mama gave Button a big smile, then left the room, closing the door softly behind her. Button snuggled down under the quilt. Despite the sore throat, it would be good to lie here under the covers and smell Mama's baking and listen to her singing as she went about her day's work. Perhaps she would make something especially good for Button since she was a sick girl. If she did, Button would try to swallow no matter how much it hurt. And Papa might play on the organ for her. He knew how much she enjoyed hearing him play and sing . . . and. . . . The door pushed open and there stood Mama.

"Button, what in the world are you doing in bed?" she asked the bewildered child, who now sat up and stared at her.

"I am sick, Mama, remember? I have a sore throat and a fever. . . . You couldn't have forgotten already. . . . I told you about it just a few minutes ago."

Mama took one step nearer Button's bed and pointed her finger at her daughter.

"You *were* sick, Button," she corrected. "You *did* have a sore throat and a fever, but no more! I prayed for you, didn't I? Get up this minute and go to school!"

Mama marched out from the room without a backward glance, and Button crawled slowly out of bed and dressed in her school clothes. She thought of her sore throat and how cold the Lapland air was. . . .

She felt sick most of the day, but she hardly dared to think about it, for that surely would be a sin after Mama had prayed for her. She shivered a little as she sat on her bench, but by the time she started home that afternoon, her sickness had left her. She simply could not return sick to the parsonage when Mama had prayed her well.

Button smiled happily as she entered the farmhouse. What a wonderful night this had turned out to be! A heavy burden had been rolled from her shoulders. God had taken her dream to keep for her until she was ready to write. No longer need she worry. It might take weeks, or months, or years . . . but in God's time her dream would be fulfilled, and she would wait even if it took a hundred years.

BOOK II

CHAPTER 7

✎ For Better or Worse

Years, thought Button, were like a broad road. Sometimes there were long stretches of straightness; again there would be twists and turns, and one could not see very far ahead. Then sometimes around a bend would be waiting a fine surprise—a golden sunset or a lovely lake.

The first years in America had been like that, so different one from another. As Button had gone through the process of growing up, Mama had looked worriedly at her because there seemed to be no thoughts of marriage in Button's mind. Mama could not understand that Button was having a good time being beaued about by many a young man, but that as yet she had not met one who in any way resembled Gunnar. Not that her heart any longer beat with rapture at the thought of him—the years had seen to that—but rather that she could not recapture the glow and sincerity and sweetness that had surrounded that first love.

And then she met Eric Bjork! Eric had been as different from Gunnar as anyone could be, but for the first time a spark of the old romance had been kindled, and her

111

heart had been warmed with a gentle yearning. That had been the beginning of a new era in her life.

At the open window white ruffled curtains fluttered in the warm summer breeze. Out in the huge oak trees birds were singing their morning songs. There must be at least a hundred of them, thought Button, as she let her head sink deeper into the soft white pillow. She lay very still so she would not awaken Eric, who slept close beside her. As she listened to his even breathing, her heart almost turned a somersault in sheer delight; she was deliriously happy in her role as wife! She could hear the lazy lapping of the tiny waves along the shore. Across the lake the White Mountains towered against the sky.

Last night she and Eric had come upon the cabin bathed in moonlight. Never would she forget the thrill she felt, as leaning over her husband's shoulder, she saw him sign their names together for the first time. *Mr. and Mrs. Eric Bjork,* he had written, then turned and grinned at her as contentedly as though he owned the whole world. Button had returned a smile so radiant it proclaimed beyond a doubt that she was the world's happiest bride. She had married the man she loved, and this was their honeymoon.

"Let's not make any plans, Eric," Button had suggested when they had discussed where they would go on their honeymoon. "We'll just get in your car and drive until we want to stop. Then we'll stay at the first tourist place we find. I bet when the people there see the happiness in our faces, they'll know we're honeymooners and offer us the very best accommodations."

"That will suit me, Button," Eric had assured her and

produced one of his rare, warm smiles that penetrated right down to her toes.

Eric was not a man of fancy words. Nor was he the tall, dark man Button had dreamed her husband would be. If anyone had told her a year ago that she would marry Eric, she would have flatly denied it. She would have said, "Eric Bjork is a fine person, kind, good-looking and perhaps a little well-to-do, but wonderful as he is, he is not the one for me!"

They had few things in common, and Eric was not one who wanted to become entangled in Button's dreams. But from the first she had enjoyed his company, feeling secure in his presence, so she saw him frequently. Soon she found she was going out only with him.

"I can't understand it," she had confided to Vickey, who at seventeen was already married. "I don't know whether or not I love him. This feeling is so different from the one I had for Gunnar in Lapland."

Vickey had patted her on the shoulder.

"Don't worry, Sister, one of these days you'll know if you love him enough to marry him, just as I did with John."

And Button did know in her heart the night he had proposed to her. They were out riding.

"Button," Eric had said as he stopped the car beside a shimmering lake, "I want to tell you something strange. Although I've been taking girls out since I was old enough, there has never been a thought of marriage in my mind. I always wanted to be a bachelor. You're the first girl I ever wanted to marry. Will you marry me?"

Button had laughed. "Why, Eric," she said, "if that is supposed to be a proposal, it certainly isn't a very romantic one. Don't you know you are supposed to sweep a girl off her feet or at least take her in your arms to demonstrate your words?"

He had looked at her for a long while and then had started the car and driven on.

"You are like all the rest," he had said finally. "In your heart, you are laughing at me. Well, I won't ask you again, Miss Franzon. If you love me, you'll have to come to me."

Without another word he had driven her to the parsonage, escorted her to the door, and driven off with such speed that Mama had called out, "What in the world, Button? Did you and Eric have a fight?"

"Oh, no, Mama . . . not at all. We're the best of friends. . . . We might even get married."

And Button had left Mama standing there just as perplexed as she herself felt. Inside she had been fuming. Why, he could not treat her like that! She would never go to him—never—never. Who did he think he was anyway?

But she found that she was thinking of him day and night and hoping that he would call again. But two weeks passed and not a sign of him. Eric was a tool designer and an exceptionally fine one, with an excellent income. He must have money in the bank, and he was rather handsome in an intent, serious way. Very rarely did his face break into a happy smile. He was of medium height with blond hair. He, too, had been born in Sweden. That was one thing they did have in common, speaking their own country's language and talking about the old country they had left behind.

"He needs me to make him happy," Button reasoned, "and I need him to keep me balanced." It would be good to find him waiting when she came back from her dream tours. Resting in his strong arms, she'd feel safe. So she waited and waited for his call, refusing to go out with other boys. And one night it came.

"Button," said his voice on the telephone, "I couldn't hold out any longer! Will you come out with me tonight and look at the house I'd like to buy for our future home?"

Eric is pretty sure of himself, she thought, but she felt very happy, so she went with him to see the little white bungalow with green shutters. To Button it was almost like seeing her dream house in Lapland. Eric was kind, but he did not speak of marriage, although his strong arms around her and his kisses told her more than words.

"Eric," Button had said that night, "you'll have to ask Papa for my hand if we are to get married. Also you'll have to join the church, for it's understood in our household that we will marry only church people, and you——"

He stopped her with a kiss. "I'll do both those things, dear. I want you, Button. Oh, I know it may be hard for me to fit into your large family or into your dreams, but somehow I must manage it. You know, Button, sometimes you seem to me like a lost bird flying around trying to find a warm nest. That's why I want to buy you a home, so you will always know where you belong."

But Eric found he could not ask Papa for Button's hand.

"I am scared!" he confessed. "And anyway, that's old-fashioned. People don't do that any more. We, you and I, are the ones who want to get married. What has Papa to do with it?"

"You'd be surprised!" laughed Button. "One thing I surely know, you don't know my Papa!"

At Eastertime Eric joined Papa's church. (Farm days

were over and Papa had gone back to his lifework.) Papa was most happy to receive Eric into the fellowship of the church, for he was convinced that Eric was sincere in joining. Eric still refused, however, to ask Papa for Button's hand, so she finally had to help him.

"Why don't you write Papa a letter, Eric?" she asked, the idea just having popped into her mind, "and if you don't know what to say, I can help you."

"That's a good idea, Button," said Eric in a relieved voice. "Write it soon, will you?"

After Button had finished the letter, she showed it to Eric:

Dear Pastor Franzon,

I am writing to ask you a great favor, the greatest I have ever asked of a human being. Button and I love each other and I would consider it the most wonderful thing in the world if I could make her my wife. I promise to be a good husband and with God's help to provide well for her. I shall count the moments until I receive your reply, which I hope will be favorable.

With deepest respect,
Eric Bjork

"Why, Button, that's a good job. I couldn't have expressed it better myself. How in the world could you do it?"

"Two things," smiled Button, "a mind and a heart. Now you must copy it in your handwriting and mail it to Papa."

It did not take Papa long to have a talk with Button and to return a favorable reply to the overjoyed Eric and by Christmas time Button wore a sparkling diamond on her finger. Eric purchased the white bungalow and the two of them spent every spare moment picking out furniture and getting ready for a June wedding. What wonderful memories these happy, happy days made.

Now Button looked over at Eric, noting his strong fine features. He was her dear husband and, happy as she was, of that she was certain. Of course, he had been pretty nervous on the wedding day, and they were both relieved when it was over. Eric was not a man who sought out the limelight, so different from her own family where each person seemed destined to be in some position that dealt with the public. Well, she would get accustomed to this new life and learn to love it. The wedding had been so beautiful! Poor Papa! Having two weddings so close, Vickey's and hers, had been hard on his purse strings, but he had not complained when he had seen the light in Button's eyes.

"After all," he had said to Button, "our family can use a man who knows how to work with his hands."

Mama, of course, had cried all through the ceremony and the tears had been streaming down her cheeks when she had kissed them good-bye.

"Be good to her, Eric," she had whispered. "I declare, she can sometimes be a pack of trouble."

Papa had shaken Eric's hand so hard Button was afraid it would fall right off.

"Eric, my son," Papa had said in his preaching voice, "you are getting one of the nicest girls that ever was born. Oh, she might be up to mischief, she always was, but your life will never be dull with Button beside you."

Dear Papa, how good he had been. Button knew that

both Papa and Mama had been a bit disappointed that she
had not married a minister. Perhaps they wondered how
she would get along in such a complete change of environ-
ment, but Eric was smart and they felt he would go a long
way in his line, and as far as worldly goods were concerned, Button would have much more than Vickey, who
had married a preacher. So Papa and Mama had given
Eric and Button their blessings with hearts overflowing.

At the close of the wedding reception Eric and Button
had slipped away to begin their honeymoon journey. Eric
was proud of his shiny new car, but they had not gone very
far when Button sitting close beside him said in a wistful
voice:

"Oh, Eric, I can't bear to think of our little dream
house being alone on our wedding night. It will have its
arms stretched out in a warm welcome, but no one will
come up that walk unless—do you think we can turn back?
I'd so much rather stay in our own home tonight and start
our trip tomorrow. Am I being foolish, Eric, when we are
already on our way? But darling, being in our own place
would be heavenly."

Eric had turned the car around and headed for home.
He was as glad as Button was to spend the first night of
his married life in his own home. Thus in the evening dusk
they had stood outside their bungalow, gazing at the red
geraniums blossoming in the window-boxes beneath the
front windows, and at the roses, which Eric had planted
that spring, climbing up the porch trellis.

Eric, full of pride, took out the new key, but Button
held him back.

"Wait, darling," she whispered. "Let's just stand here

and take it all in for a few minutes and then, as we walk toward the door, hold me very, very close."

She needed his comforting arms around her as she started this new life. What would it be like? Would she always be as happy as this? Would they have little ones running around in this house, pressing their noses against the windowpanes? Would Eric learn to smile more, and would she be the good wife she wanted to be? As Eric opened the door, they stopped.

"Would you think me queer, if I asked that we kneel, Eric?" Button asked.

"Not at all, honey! I'll do anything to make you happy," answered Eric, holding her hand tightly in his.

Button remembered Mama telling how she and Papa had knelt at the threshhold before entering their home in Lapland when they had returned as newlyweds. She had always wanted to do the same. They knelt and prayed silently that God would bless them and everyone who entered their door. Then Eric carried her across the threshold and kissed her tenderly.

"Welcome home, Mrs. Bjork!" he said with a strange catch in his husky voice.

Certainly everything had been perfect, blessings unnumbered were pouring down upon them. She was sure Eric would be the kindest and most thoughtful husband in the whole world.

Now, lying here in the big bed in the log cabin, she remembered how Eric and she had wandered through their home that night before last, and she had touched each new thing caressingly. They had planned where to place the numerous wedding presents that would add so much to their new home. How spotlessly clean their house was!

They must always keep it so—no discord, no ugly words, no complaints, no criticism . . . just joy and love and laughter for years and years until eternity began.

So they crept into their new mahogany bed whispering lovers' sweet nothings to each other. Button had bubbled over with words.

"Darling," she murmured with her check pressed close against her husband's, "promise me you'll live to be a hundred and eleven years old, because I could never think of life without you, Eric."

He laughed heartily.

"Why do you laugh?" Button asked, a tiny bit annoyed.

"Oh, I was thinking that you would be a hundred and three that fall—and a picture flashed through my mind of how you would look."

"Now that wasn't even kind of you, Eric," she scolded, "and surely not a bit romantic. Don't you know that to you I shall always be beautiful because love is ageless? Oh, Eric, Eric, you must learn to say pretty things to me. And do you know what? I would simply fold up and die if you stopped loving me!"

Eric kissed the frown from her forehead and held her so close she could hear his heart beating wildly.

"Honey," he said seriously, "you'll have to learn to accept me as I am, and I am not a man of flowery words. I am not capable of feeding you those pretty phrases you seem to crave. It's too hard for me to get them out, Button. I want you to understand this about me from the beginning. But, dear, you will learn that there are other ways beside words in which a man shows his beloved that he loves her. Love is also measured by the way he acts and what he does for her."

"Thank you for telling me, Eric, the first night. That was very wise of you. Now I will understand you, so please, don't worry about it."

In the morning they had driven toward the White Mountains in beautiful, picturesque New Hampshire, and that night in the moonlight they had seen the vacancy sign on the log cabin by the big lake. They both felt they must have been divinely led to this spot, for they couldn't have found a prettier place to spend their honeymoon.

Yes, life was wonderful and Eric would make a fine husband and father. God would bless them as He had blessed Papa and Mama. Button touched Eric lightly on the cheek.

"Wake up sleepyhead," she whispered. "It's morning! Even a hundred and eleven years are too short to live if we're going to waste them sleeping."

Eric reached out his arms and drew her close. "Already you have become a very disturbing wife. But you are as adorable as you are crazy. I know now what your Papa meant when he said my life would never be dull living with his daughter!"

That first year was heavenly, and there certainly wasn't one dull moment. To Button marriage was far more than she had ever dreamed it could be. Every day Eric became dearer, and she learned that underneath his reserved manner he hid much goodness. It shone out in so many little ways, but most of all Button felt secure in his strength. Yes, Eric and she belonged together. God had made them for each other. He was a perfect husband, and they would sail through life on a calm sea and someday there would be children to share their happiness. Button needed only to close her eyes and she could hear the sound of children's voices. In her mind she had already turned one of the rooms into a dainty nursery. Tired as he was, Eric would come home with a glow on his face and stop in the kitchen doorway while she flew into his outstretched arms. Life would always be like this for them even when they were both old. She would keep it this way and would never lose the thrill of feeling that pressure of his fingers which he had told her meant, "I love you, darling." No, they would always treasure this perfect happiness which hovered over their home like a thousand angel wings.

In those first few months, with Mama as her teacher, Button learned to be a good housekeeper. And Mama also told her how to handle a husband the right way.

"One of the most important things," Mama had advised as they sat in the sunshine on Button's front step one clear October afternoon when Mama had come for lunch, "is always to have the dinner ready when your man comes home from work. Have the table set as perfectly as though you expected company, the silver straight, and a centerpiece of flowers or something green. This adds so much to the meal. You see, Button dear, it's the small things that make a house into a home. Eric should smell rolls baking and coffee percolating as he comes up the walk at night. He should know that loving arms will greet him and that busy hands have prepared everything for his comfort. Thus he can leave his burdens outside the door and forget his weariness from the strain of work. He should feel that here he is king and this his castle."

"I love to hear you tell me these things, Mama. I guess

a woman who does all those things will never lose her husband's love."

"No, of that I am sure," continued Mama happily, "and don't forget, my dear, that the nicest music to a hungry man's ears is the clatter of pots and pans in the kitchen. It makes a man feel important. God made him that way so never blame him for it. When you promised in your marriage vow to reverence your husband, it did not mean that you would gaze at him adoringly night and day as some people do at a preacher in the pulpit. No, it meant that you would darn his socks, wash and starch his shirts, have his meals ready and give him plenty to eat. Also it meant that you would keep yourself clean and pleasant-smelling, using a little touch of perfume behind the ear on the side of the face you turn toward him to kiss."

"Oh, Mama, you are so clever. I'll never forget your advice."

Button was especially glad she had not married a minister so she would have had to live in a parsonage the way Vickey did . . . even if Vickey thought that was part of heaven.

"It takes a lot of living to make a house a homey place, Button," insisted Vickey. "Just think of the generations of people who must have lived in this old parsonage. Here people have laughed and cried for almost a hundred years. Its wooden arms have sheltered them in joy and through sorrow. It possesses character, style, memories. I'm not a bit envious of your new bungalow."

"But our house belongs to us, Vickey! Someday it too will be old, but we are the ones to begin its story. Here we came on our wedding night. We were the first to ask God's blessing upon it. Here I cooked our first meal and in time, here I'll hold our first baby in my arms. And it is small—so small that when we're away from it, we can hold it in the palm of one hand. We will have years and years to pour our love into it."

Well, they were both contented and satisfied with what they had, and that was the important thing. Every object in their homes was hallowed, and how could it be otherwise when in each all was peace and joy and love?

There was something Button had carried with her from Sweden that she wished she could have left behind. It was a sense of fear about America. People there had told her hair-raising stories of murders, kidnapings and burglaries which happened all the time. She had tried to drive these stories from her mind, but on nights when Eric worked very late, they came back to haunt her. One day she read about an axe murder which had taken place in their community, and although she did not mention it to Eric, she was almost overcome with fear. What would stop a man like that from coming into their little home in the silence of the night and murdering them both? She knew it was a horrid thought, and that Eric would be very cross if he knew that she let things like that take possession of her mind. She tried to think of happy things, but when she was alone, her mind would wander back to the murder and she would shake like a leaf. Her imagination built the fear up more and more. It was best to be on guard at all times. But how? So the idea came to her. No one would be able to sneak up on Eric and her as they were peacefully sleeping in their bed if she secured the door. The next day Button purchased a large brass hook and ring from the hardware store and fastened them in their proper places.

She wondered what Eric would say about it. She wouldn't tell him, but would hook the door after he was in bed. If he happened to catch her, she'd just have to explain that she hadn't been able to sleep because of the fear that possessed her. Eric would surely pamper her about the hook . . . he had to.

Eric did not see Button slipping the hook on the door that night, but in the morning they were awakened by a severe thunder storm. She had awakened before Eric, having enjoyed undisturbed sleep for the first time in weeks. She was lying in bed thinking that the hook really did not detract too much from the look of the door when Eric opened his eyes and spotted it.

"Button," he cried, "how did that hook get on the door?"

"I put it there," said Button meekly.

"Do you mean to tell me that you hammered a huge hook into our expensive woodwork? How could you do a thing like that and what in the world for?"

Never before had Button heard Eric speak to her in that tone of voice. Her heart sank. Perhaps he would not understand after all. Better tell him the truth.

"I put it there so we wouldn't be murdered at night when we were sleeping. I've been terribly frightened ever since the axe murder. I had to do something!"

Eric sat up in bed. He was furious.

"Are you implying that I am not capable of protecting you? Do you think I am a mouse? And there you are sleeping right beside me! What do you think people will think when they see that hook? They'll think I am as frightened as you! It's ridiculous. I shall remove it at once."

"You will do nothing of that kind, Mr. Bjork. When

other couples get murdered in their beds, you'll thank God you had a wife smart enough to take precautions against it. If you touch that hook, I'll walk out of this house and never come back!"

"O. K. I suppose that hook will have to stay. It will remain as a symbol of the disgrace of my manhood and the foolishness of your womanhood. It has been like that since Adam and Eve. A woman loves to make a fool of a man."

Button stared at her husband. The stinging tears were hard to keep back, but she wouldn't allow herself to cry. She looked at him with eyes full of hurt pride and contempt. "I think you are horrid!" she blurted out.

Eric neither answered nor looked her way. He dressed quickly, walked through the hall and kitchen, and, without eating breakfast, he opened the door and slammed it hard behind him. Not a word of good-bye had come from him.

Button dressed slowly. She let the tears fall now. Her whole beautiful dream world had tumbled down. Everything was spoiled. The ugly words had come, their house was not the same . . . would never be the same. Eric was not perfect! He was very human and had a terrible temper. No one in the parsonage would ever have walked out like that, or if he did, a few minutes later he would have been on his knees, asking God's and the injured one's forgiveness. Now everything she considered sacred in their home had been desecrated by Eric's act. What should she do?

Button searched her own heart carefully and honestly. Could she help it if she was frightened by the gruesome things she read in the newspaper? Wasn't it Eric's duty to love and understand . . . for better or worse?

Then suddenly a wild desire to write came over her. Soon her pen was flying over the paper at a furious rate, the words coming so fast she had a hard time holding them back. The story she wrote was about a young girl who thought she had married a perfect man but after a year of married life discovered his imperfections. There had been a big quarrel about a minor thing, and the husband had left the house without eating his breakfast or kissing the wife good-bye, and he had slammed the door behind him. The young wife was sitting in her living room thinking of what an ill-tempered, inconsiderate, selfish brute of a male she had married when the door bell rang twice. Carefully wiping the tears from her eyes, she had opened the door and there on the steps stood a boy with a big box, which he handed her. Upon opening it, she found it contained two dozen beautiful red roses.

"Oh, my husband is sorry he hurt me this morning," the wife said to herself while all the bitterness she had felt completely vanished away. "This is his way of saying that he wants me to forgive him. Now I must go him one better. I'm not going to let him know that the flowers have come, but I'll telephone him to say how sorry I am for my part in the argument . . . I'll admit I was wrong . . . I'll forgive him and he'll be happy again—thanks to the red roses."

The husband seemed very surprised when she called him, but they made up and all was well. In a few minutes she would call him back and thank him for the roses. As she put back the receiver, the bell rang again, and there stood the same boy looking flushed and embarrassed.

"L-l-lady," he stammered, "will you forgive the awful mistake I made in delivering the roses to you? I lost the card and thought I remembered the correct house number, but I just found the card and I should have given them to the lady next door."

As Button wrote, time and space were forgotten and even the unhappiness Eric had caused her dissolved into thin air. All her clouds had vanished and once again she was basking beneath a blue heaven. After the story was finished (and she had given it a happy ending), she placed it in an envelope and mailed it to a magazine. Perhaps, after all, this was a day of good luck, and she had needed a jolt to make her write a story.

After the envelope was mailed, she took courage and called Eric.

"Eric," she said sweetly, "this is the naughty girl you married a year ago. . . . I got lonesome for my husband."

"Is that because there is a bad man in the house?" he asked teasingly, but he was laughing, and Button knew his anger had gone.

"I've removed the hook, Eric, and filled in the holes with plastic wood. Then I rubbed some polish over the spots and they are hardly noticeable. Am I forgiven?"

"Of course! After all, since this was my wife's first offense, I'll have to be lenient. But you'll have to promise not to tear down my manly pride again!"

"I promise, Eric, and there'll be steak waiting tonight. Why don't you ask your boss to come for dinner? Don't tell him I suggested it, and will he be surprised when he sees what a delicious meal I've prepared. He'll wish he wasn't a bachelor and will propose to the first girl he sees just to get a wife—after having had a sample of your wife's cooking!"

"Perhaps I will ask Mr. Nord, Button. He may think that we have steaks every meal! But let me tell you something, Mrs. Bjork, you are the world's biggest schemer. . . . But I don't mind as long as your schemes include a steak."

Button hung up the receiver The world was fine again. She was sure her story would sell. She would, indeed, cook the biggest steak her money would buy for Mr. Nord and her husband.

CHAPTER 8

❧ The Angel

Button's story was accepted by the small magazine to which she had sent it, and she received a check for five dollars with the request for further stories of a similar type. This made her so happy she felt as if she were dancing on clouds. With the money she bought a heavy doorstop which she told Eric would always stand by their bedroom door as a reminder to her not to fasten any more hooks on it.

The first year of their marriage had flown by as swiftly as if it had wings, and again it was summer. Eric and Button, with Vickey and John, had rented a summer cottage for two weeks. The White Mountains had been the choice of Eric and Button, since there they could relive their honeymoon days. The two weeks were much too short, and Button found it unbearable to think of going back to the city heat.

"I still have two more weeks' vacation," said John a couple of days before their time was up. "If this place hasn't been rented, why don't we stay another two weeks and you, Eric, could drive up for weekends? It may be hard on you, but at least it would give you two long weekends here."

130

"Poor Eric," sighed Button. "That's the only time I wish you were a preacher, when vacation comes around."

"I'll live through it," laughed Eric, who looked brown and rested, "and it will be wonderful for you, Button. Let's go and ask if we can have it for two more weeks!"

They returned with good news and settled down for another two weeks of stimulating mountain air.

Without Eric the week seemed endless to Button and when Friday night finally came, she announced that she would walk up the road to meet her husband. She couldn't wait to be in his arms again. She tied a bandana tightly around her hair. A fine rain was falling, but the clouds were breaking and it looked as if the rain might cease at any moment. Darkness was beginning to fall like a dark veil over the woodland, so Button walked fast. Now and then a bird chirped, and far in the distance a dog was barking. From the lake came the gay voices of young people who were swimming despite the rain and darkness. Oh, how Button longed for the sound of Eric's car! He simply must come before it got too dark or how would she find her way back without a flashlight? How foolish of her to have forgotten to take one along. But she walked bravely on, for surely Eric would come at any moment, and he would be proud to see that she had walked all this way by herself just to meet him. She must have walked at least a full mile.

This was a very special night! So special that only God in heaven and she knew the importance of it. She sat down by the edge of the road to rest awhile, drinking in the scent of fresh pine. Would Eric be glad to hear the news? And how was she to break it to him? She could say, "Eric, the most wonderful thing in the world has happened to us—the miracle of the ages from the beginning of time. . . .

We—you and I are going to be parents—and do you know what? . . . It's going to be a Christmas present or a New Year's one anyway. Isn't it wonderful?"

Or perhaps she should just put her arms around his neck and kiss him and whisper, "I am about to become the mother of your first-born, Mr. Bjork!"

Or better yet, she could just look deep into his eyes and let him read the secret in hers, for by now she was sure it was written all over her face. A joy like hers could not be concealed.

It had been a strain to wait all these weeks to tell him, but she had wanted to be absolutely sure first, and Mama had said, "When you feel life, then you are sure, Button." She had shared her news with Mama, Vickey and Greta— but Eric—well—she had wanted to be without a doubt before she told him.

And now, just today, it had happened. Button had been having a good swim in the cool, clear water and had sat down on the dock to dry off. A beautiful bluebird had flown to a branch not far from where she was sitting. It sat there looking down upon her, and then, for the first time, she felt something stir within her, like the lifting of a tiny finger—then it felt more pronounced like a tiny ball rolling over. Oh, it had brought tears to Button's eyes and she had offered a prayer of thanksgiving for her happiness. Then she had gone up to the cottage to tell Vickey. Button had stood there gazing into Vickey's blue eyes and then embraced her sister.

"Vickey," she cried, "I felt it! It is real! So tiny—but it let me know it really is there. I'm so happy I could die!"

And Vickey had kissed her. "God bless you!" she had whispered.

It had seemed to Button that night would never come. With night would come Eric and she would tell him her secret and need no longer keep it locked in her heart.

The rain had stopped. A lone bird twittered in the tall treetop. The air felt fresh and pure. She took a deep breath and filled her lungs with mountain air. "For my little one," she smiled.

From now on she would always think of that new little life first. How much she loved it already! And now Eric, too, could share this new love. She could hear a car coming down the twisting road. Her heart almost stopped with joy! It was he! It was Eric! She tore off her bandana and waved it. Eric stopped the car and opened the door.

"Hi! How about a lift for a tired hiker?" she laughed.

"Why, Button, how did you dare to venture this far into the woods by yourself? But it's a very pleasant surprise, indeed."

She seated herself close beside him and he kissed her hungrily.

"I had to meet you, Eric. I was terribly lonesome!"

"That's fine, honey. I like to have you get lonesome for your husband."

They drove in silence thankful to be together again.

Then, "Eric, don't you think it would be nice for me to have a little son to walk with me?"

Eric laughed. "No," he said teasingly, "positively not. I don't want any competition—at least not for many years."

Button's heart stood still with fear. Eric did not want a baby! How could she tell him now? Why had he spoiled it all? Her sensitive, foolish heart ached and her throat was full of crying. She pulled herself away from him, almost hugging the door.

"I don't care what you want, Eric," she blurted out. "You are going to have a baby whether you want one or not—because—because—there isn't a thing we can do about it now."

Eric slammed on the brakes. "Button, you silly little girl! Do you realize we almost had an accident? Do you think that's a kind way to break such news to an expectant father? Do you really mean it, dearest? Are you sure? I couldn't take it if you were fooling me!"

There were tears in Eric's eyes—real tears—and Button felt that she had reached a joy so divine it could not belong to this earth alone.

The world became topsy-turvy. Everything was centered around one thing, the baby . . . December . . . Christmas! Eric was the most tender expectant father Button had ever seen. It was as if he had been transformed, all the mirth that had been held back by his reserved nature suddenly exploded. He was a happy man!

Button forgot about her writing. This new experience so completely dominated her that she poured every ounce of her strength into creating a nursery so beautiful and sweet that it would have been fit for a prince. For the little white crib she embroidered a bedspread, showing diminutive angels showering roses down from a blue sky. Weeks of work went into the scarf that covered the small bureau and into the white ruffled curtains which were tied back with wide pink satin ribbons.

Eric bought a daybed for the nursery, saying to Button, "For you, darling. I know you'll want to be near the baby when you first come home from the hospital; it will be so helpless then, you won't want to leave it alone."

Button made some fluffy pillows to throw upon the bed so it would not look so large amid the baby things. Three months before she was due to have the baby all was in readiness and the nursery became to her almost as sacred as a shrine. Each day she knelt and prayed by the little crib, asking that the new life might be healthy and happy and good.

Then Button had to face her first disappointment in connection with the nursery. There was to be a big convention held in Papa's church and delegates would be coming from near and far. Thus Mama came on a special errand to see Button on a sunny November morning.

"Button," said Mama, as she sat drinking coffee in her daughter's spotless kitchen, "I informed the convention committee yesterday that I knew that you and Eric would be glad to take one of the delegates for a couple of nights. We have so many people coming that we have to make use of every available place. Everyone who has a space at all has volunteered to take at least one guest. We are having seven in the parsonage for four days. Your guest will be an elderly farm lady, and I'm sure she will just love to sleep in your little nursery."

Button, her eyes getting bigger and bigger, stared at Mama. "Mama, you can't mean that! Not that we shall ask an old lady to sleep in our baby's nursery."

"Oh, she won't mind that it is a nursery, Button. She'll be grateful to have so nice a place to stay."

"Well, I should say SHE won't mind." Button was so upset she could hardly speak. "I should say SHE would be very comfortable, indeed, only she's not going to be; no one is going to sleep in the nursery until the baby has slept in it first."

Mama looked at Button a long time without answering, but under her steady gaze Button lived through the years of her childhood. She saw the endless line of people who had been guests in the parsonage. A strange crowd of crippled and sick ones, but also those happy and well. She knew that Mama never closed the door to anyone as long as there was one place left to crowd someone in, and she always served her guests the best the house could afford. That was Mama's way of serving God.

Finally Mama smiled. "Button," she said kindly, "I'm sure you're not a foolish, selfish girl. You certainly are not going to keep an old lady from realizing her dreams of coming to the convention because of your emotionalism over an unborn baby. Think upon this seriously before you reply. But, little one, let me tell you that there will be a special blessing coming to you if you open your home to Mrs. Frankenberg."

Button lived through agony until Eric came home from work. He found her snuggled up on the daybed in the nursery, her eyes red with weeping, and no supper prepared. Sobbing, she threw herself into his arms and told him the whole story. The lines on Eric's forehead deepened as he tried to solve this new problem.

"Never mind, Button," he finally said. "Dry your tears and let old Mrs. Frankenberg come. That is better than to have trouble with Mama. You know very well that if Mama has made up her mind that we are going to have that old woman in our nursery, no power on earth can stop her."

"But, Eric, it is so unfair! This is OUR house and OUR baby and OUR nursery. Mama has no right to interfere."

Eric took his handkerchief and wiped away the falling tears and in no time he had convinced her that there was no other way out of this situation but to cater to Mama's wishes.

Mrs. Frankenberg proved to be a very happy, talkative old lady and because she lived in the country she was delighted with all the things of the city.

"I'm going to spend as much time at the meetings as I need to bring back a report to our church," she informed Button, "but I'm also going to do all my Christmas shopping. I was pretty lucky to have been chosen delegate from our group. It has never happened before."

"I'm glad you could come," replied Button, wondering if she was telling a lie, though she really felt better about the whole affair now that she saw how truly delighted the old lady was.

Mrs. Frankenberg was thrilled with all the wonderful things she could buy in the Berkley Hills stores, and she came home with bundle after bundle. Button wondered if she got to church at all.

One afternoon Mrs. Frankenberg unwrapped a package that contained the softest white flannel cloth Button had ever seen and yards and yards of delicate, rare lace.

"This is for nightgowns for my two sisters," the old lady confided to Button. "They're both large women, so I bought plenty. Did you ever see flannel so soft as this? I simply couldn't resist it."

Button admitted she hadn't.

"I'll have plenty of time to sew it before the holidays, and can't you just see the gowns with this lovely lace? I know two women who are going to be very lucky this Christmas Day. By the way, do you mind if I don't wrap it up for a while? I get pleasure just looking at it from my bed. May I leave it in the crib on top of all those angels? . . . See, I bought scissors, pins and thread and I'm all set to go."

What could Button do but say that was all right? She had never met a person who could get so enthused over little things. Well, the nursery was lived in now, so what difference would it make if Mrs. Frankenberg placed the cloth in the crib?

Mama had more requests. The hard-working church women needed a bit of extra help for their luncheon the next day. They would not let Mama help because she had her hands full with so many guests, but would Button go down and help with a sit-down job, like buttering rolls? It would take some of the burden off the few who were working.

Button left her house at nine the next morning. Mama had been so happy that she had said yes. Mrs. Frankenberg decided to do a bit more shopping before the last meeting.

With Button's house empty, Mama had her own plans. Last night she had obtained a key from Eric, remembering the special blessing she had promised Button. God was a little slow at times in bestowing His blessings, and Mama wanted Button to see that her words were true. She would help God out today, and since she didn't have to be at church until afternoon, she had time to go to Button's house and make her a nice daffodil cake and frost it with fluffy cream icing. Button would love that and she could put in a *brun peparkaka,* too, just for good measure.

It was fun to be in Eric's and Button's immaculate home and to putter around in the kitchen. Before Mama started her baking, she tiptoed into the nursery. Poor Button, it had been hard for her to give in, but it was good for her. Young people of today were apt to think only of themselves, and when it came to her own, she had better nip that trait in the bud. Her eyes rested upon the little white crib and its bundle of soft white flannel.

"Why," she said aloud to herself, "think of that, Button is going to attempt to sew baby clothes! The way she sews this lovely flannel will be ruined in no time at all. . . . Such beautiful lace, too."

An idea popped into Mama's head. Instead of making a cake, why not make the baby clothes? She could do it in no time at all on Button's sewing machine, whereas it would take Button forever. Mama was an excellent sewer, and wouldn't Button be happy when she saw a pile of baby clothes all finished! Button would know she really had received a blessing for accepting Mrs. Frankenberg.

In a few hours the task was completed. Mama smiled impishly as she folded the little nighties, shirts and diapers, three piles of them. If Button had spent months at it, they wouldn't have looked as well. There was one yard of material left, and Mama spread it over the clothes and placed on top the scissors and thread and the strip of lace that was left over. It looked as before. She would not tell Button until tomorrow when Mrs. Frankenberg had gone home. What a surprise!

Mr. Frankenberg came home late in the afternoon, tired from attending meetings and Christmas shopping.

"I got it done! I got it done! Every last bit of it. Not one Christmas present left to buy. But"—she looked pleadingly at Button—"would you mind if I stayed one more night and left in the morning. I would have to rush so to catch that bus now."

"Of course, you may stay, Mrs. Frankenberg. Have a good night's rest, and I'll wake you early in the morning. That will be so much better."

What else could she say, even though the old lady had worn out her welcome a long time ago? Tomorrow it would be all over, and she could clean the nursery and put her home in order the way it had been before the guest arrived. Her stay had not been too bad after all.

The next morning she woke Mrs. Frankenberg as soon as Eric had left for work. She cooked her a nice, big breakfast, to send her off with pleasant memories since she was their first overnight guest and was not responsible for Button's own attitude toward the nursery.

Mrs. Frankenberg was all sunshine. She appeared in a red robe she had bought. "If you excuse me, this robe is so warm and pretty-looking, I thought I would eat first and pack afterwards," she said, her eyes feasting on the delicious-looking ham omelet Button was placing on the table.

"Have a good breakfast now," Button smiled. "You'll have plenty of time to pack and get ready. The bus is just down the hill, you know."

"I don't know how I'm ever going to thank you. I've been so comfortable in that darling nursery. I wish you lots of luck with your first one. The child will be very lucky having you for a mother. How can I ever repay you for your kindness to an old lady?"

"Oh, don't even think about it, Mrs. Frankenberg," assured Button. "It has already been paid for."

Mrs. Frankenberg took another piece of coffee bread.

"You mean the church will pay for me?" she asked bluntly.

"Oh, no, I didn't mean that kind of payment. There are other ways you get repaid for the little things you do for others. Mama calls it a special blessing."

"Well, I'm glad to hear that," laughed the old lady. "You see, I had intended to buy some little thing for you and Eric, something to remember me by, but with all the Christmas buying I did, my money just melted like snow in hot water. But you'll be glad to know that all my shopping is done, every bit of it, and on top of that I have a lot of good preaching tucked away in my heart. I've had a great time."

Button washed the breakfast dishes. She was glad that Mrs. Frankenberg was so pleased with her first conference and her visit. It left a rather special glow on the nursery. She felt a bit ashamed now to think that it had taken both Mama and Eric to persuade her to accept the old lady.

It was strangely quiet in the nursery, so quiet that Button wondered if Mrs. Frankenberg had gone back to bed and would ask to remain another day. Heaven forbid! If she did, Button would just have to tell her, in a nice way that this would have to be all, at least for this time.

Presently the door to the nursery opened and out stepped Mrs. Frankenberg with a suitcase in one hand and an umbrella in the other. Her hat was pushed down over her eyes and her mouth was set in a hard thin line. She marched right by Button without looking at her, and her heels made a clicking sound as she walked through the hall. At the front door she stopped and drew a deep breath. She placed her suitcase on the floor and put her free hand on her hip. Her eyes bored through Button's with a murderous look. Then without one word of explanation she opened the door, walked out, and closed it with a bang.

For a minute Button stood as if transfixed, staring at the closed door. She searched her mind to see if she had said or done something that could have offended her guest to such a degree that she had become like a thundercloud. Button could recall nothing, but she couldn't let her guest go off like that. Something was wrong, desperately wrong. She put on her coat and hurried after Mrs. Frankenberg and soon she caught up with her.

"Mrs. Frankenberg," she called, and puffed from running in her heavy condition. "Please, Mrs. Frankenberg, I'd like to walk with you to the bus and carry your suitcase. What has happened! Is something wrong?"

The old lady stopped and put down her suitcase. She pushed her hat away from her eyes, which were red from crying, and again she gave Button one of those looks that made her cringe. In a voice loaded with contempt, she said, "I owe you neither a good-bye nor a thank you, my dear Mrs. Bjork. As you told me, you have your own way of abstracting payment from a poor woman who was invited to stay at your house as a member of the church of God. A very lovely minister's daughter you are! I want neither your help nor your company for that might cost me my new red bathrobe. Who knows? And now may I bid you farewell and a very merry Christmas?"

Button went back to the house. The old lady was a lunatic. She was crazy as a loon, and here she had been staying right in their home. All sorts of things could have happened. Well, what a relief to have her gone. Now to open all the windows and let in some fresh air! Wait until she told Eric! He would be furious. She herself felt as if someone had thrown a pail of cold water over her.

The telephone rang and Button was relieved to hear Mama's happy voice.

"Are you tired, Button?" asked Mama sweetly.

"A little," confessed Button. "And happy that Mrs. Frankenberg has gone. Mama, something is wrong with that woman's mind."

"Mrs. Frankenberg's? Oh, no, she's a bit eccentric, but she has a heart of gold and is harmless. Living alone in the country may make a person a bit queer at times."

"Not just a little queer! I am at my wits' end trying to understand her actions."

"Let's forget her, darling. I called to see if you found the surprise—the special blessing that was coming your way."

"I'm afraid not, Mama. Mrs. Frankenberg just left."

"Well, look in the crib, dear."

Mama remained on the phone while Button looked. The first thing she saw was that Mrs. Frankenberg had forgotten her beautiful, soft flannel. She went to the crib and lifted it . . . and then stood with her mouth open staring at the three piles of the loveliest, darlingest baby things. For a moment she was going to hug them to her heart when she suddenly realized what Mama was about to tell her.

She dashed back to the phone. "Mama," she cried, "oh, Mama, you sewed up all the flannel!"

"Yes, Button, that is your blessing for being good. I went over to your house yesterday while you were working at the church. I intended to make you a daffodil cake, but I discovered the flannel and knew you were about to make baby clothes, so I made them up for you, little one, with lots of love tucked into every stitch. I hope you are pleased."

"Mama, Mama! Oh, dear! Poor Mrs. Frankenberg!" And Button started to laugh uncontrollably.

Mama could not stop her, no matter how she tried, so she put down the receiver and had Papa drive with her to Button's house where she learned the whole story. Mama and Papa both laughed at the strange twist Mama's blessing had taken.

"No wonder the poor dear was as mad as a hornet," said Button seriously. "She believes *I* took that flannel in payment for her lodging. And she was so delighted with that material she had bought to make nightgowns for her sisters. Now I can forgive her with all my heart."

The very next day Mama bought new material for Mrs. Frankenberg and Papa drove the thirty-five miles to her farm so Mama and Button could explain the error. Even Mrs. Frankenberg had to see the humor in the situation, and she, too, had a hearty laugh so everything turned out well with the blessing.

Early December was extremely cold that year. But in the middle of the month Button awoke one night to hear the rain beating against the windowpanes. At last the cold weather must be easing up, she thought, only to awake the following morning to a world coated with ice. Silvery icicles hung from every tree and bush, and the street and sidewalks looked like a polished dance floor. It was a fairyland sight unbelievable in its beauty, but Button's heart sank as she beheld the splendor. She had been invited to Vickey's for lunch, but how could she get there in her condition? This was the fifteenth day of the eighth month of her pregnancy, and it was hard enough to walk across the floor, let alone on the ice!

Eric must have read her thoughts, for as they were dressing he said, "Button, one promise for today. Stay inside like a bird in its nest, for it's very slippery out. If you step out, you might fall, and you mustn't do anything that might injure either the baby or yourself."

Cleverly Button avoided giving a direct answer.

"My husband is very, very wise," she recited, "and very strict. How would I dare to disobey him?"

Eric was satisfied with her answer, not knowing what was going on in his wife's mind. I did not actually say I wouldn't go out, she was thinking, but I made him think I wouldn't. He doesn't understand how important it is that I see Vickey's new baby and finish the last stitches on the carriage robe. Nothing can happen to me. I won't let it. I'll be very careful when I walk."

As Eric was ready to leave for work, he repeated his words. "Remember, no going out, Button. Have you everything you need for the day in the house?"

Button nodded her head. "Our baby is very happy this morning," she smiled, "and so excited, knowing it will be only a short while before it meets Father and Mother in person. Oh, Eric, we can count the days now!"

She blew him a kiss as the car backed out of the driveway. It skidded back and forth. How slippery it must be! thought Button, remembering Eric's words of warning to her.

Button hurried through her work. She must leave early so she would be home in plenty of time before Eric returned from work. The bus was only down the hill. It would be cozy to spend the day in Vickey's homey par-

sonage, and Littlemont was only half an hour away by bus.
A big fire would be burning in the fireplace, and Vickey's
calm personality and sweet charm would be soothing on a
wintry day such as this. They would talk of the latest things
that had been going on in the family, go on to little happenings in John's church, and end up comparing husbands
as they always did, each claiming she had the better one.
Of course, it would only be in fun. There were never two
sisters closer to each other's hearts.

As Button dressed, she stood a moment before the
mirror. She was round as a ball now, but soon her body
would yield up its fruit and she would look normal again
and have a sweet little baby sleeping in the nursery. Only a
short time now—two more weeks, and they would pass
swiftly.

"You little rascal," she whispered to the child within
her. "You dear, darling, little rascal. I love you as much as
a mother can love a baby, and I can hardly wait to see you
and say 'hello.' What do you look like? Are you a husky
boy or a tiny, cute little girl? Whatever you are, please
hurry and come to us."

It was very icy, and Button walked slowly, using special care with each step. As she came to the hill, she
stopped. Again she could hear Eric's voice. His words rang
in her ears pleadingly. She never knew Eric could be so concerned over her welfare. Should she turn back and telephone Vickey? But the day would be so long! Slowly she
started down the hill. She was over halfway down when
her feet went out from under her and she tumbled over and
over until she came to rest against a telephone pole. She
tried to ignore the fall. She tried to laugh. How comical a

sight she must be lying there like a huge snowball! But instead of laughter, crying came and the tears ran uncontrollably down her cheeks. She was very, very frightened. She couldn't get up, the sidewalk was too icy and she too heavy. Friendly people came and saw her predicament. She was carried into the home of a neighbor, who, at Button's request, called Doctor Davis.

He came immediately and shook his gray head. "You've had a bad fall, Button. I must call the ambulance and get you to the hospital. I'll call Eric at once."

"Oh, no, Doctor Davis, don't call Eric. Call Mama."

"Suppose you leave this to me," responded Doctor Davis. "We're not playing a game, and I think I know what I am doing. I know what is best in this case."

Button insisted no more. "I'm sorry, Doctor Davis," she said humbly, trying not to cry . . . trying not to think that something could have happened to the baby.

Eric came to the hospital in his working clothes. His face was drawn and his eyes sad. His hands were black, but he did not apologize, nor did he tell her, "I asked you not to go out."

It would have been so much better if he had scolded her or asked questions. He just sat there in silence, holding her hand and stroking it softly now and then.

Button stayed in the hospital a week before the baby was born. All was so strangely quiet within her. She prayed in desperation, "Please God, don't let anything be wrong with the baby. . . . I was foolish as I have been so many times . . . but Eric is so good. . . . Please, God . . . don't punish Eric." But she felt as if her prayers were not reaching God. They only went as far as the ceiling and

then fell flat on the floor. How could she pray, when she
had deliberately gone out on the icy street and fallen with
the baby that had been entrusted to her?

On the eighth day the pains began, and shortly after
that Button lost consciousness. She did not know what was
going on or whether it took hours, days or weeks. Once it
seemed as though she heard Papa's voice and Mama whispering her name. . . . Someone was crying, and she
longed to reach out her hand to tell them not to cry over a
fate she deserved . . . but she couldn't move . . . she
couldn't see. She thought Eric had touched her nose—he
had a certain little way of doing it—but she wasn't sure. . . .
All was darkness, fear and pain.

When Button finally awoke, Eric was sitting beside
her. He looked thin and worn, but he smiled and caressed
her cheek. She wanted to ask about the baby, but there was
something in Eric's face that made her afraid to. She
smiled and, holding his hand, drifted off to the silent world
again.

A month had gone by and Button was home in her
bungalow again. A strange, empty house without the nursery. There was a desk where the crib had been and on it
stood a shiny new typewriter. The spread with the angels
and roses was gone, too, and the daybed had a bright blue
slipcover. Greta had moved in to help around the house.
There were flowers and candy and books—everything that
anyone could think of—but no baby. And no one spoke
about it. Her baby girl had died, died because of a careless
mother.

Button had lost her smile. Day after day she sat in the
big chair by the living-room window doing nothing but

looking wistfully far away until late afternoon when, following the doctor's orders, she would walk down to the corner of the street and back again. She ate whatever was placed before her, but she could taste nothing because of a dryness that left her throat hot and sore. She talked very little and asked no questions, but inside her heart there were burning questions. How had her baby looked? Had it been deformed because of the fall?

Tenderly and lovingly her family sorrowed with her. She was surrounded by their love and kindness; their sweet concern made her feel as if her heart would break. She tried to eat dinner with Eric, and one day she decided to try to prepare his meals the next day. Somehow she had to fight her way back to life for Eric's sake. Time went faster if she was busy, so she thanked Greta for her kindness and asked her to go back to the parsonage. Greta gave her big sister a hug and an understanding smile—Button was alone again.

Then one day Button walked into what had been the nursery. The only things left to remind her of it were the wide satin ribbons around the curtains. Where had the nursery things been placed—the crib, the bureau, the bedspread with all the angels . . . tiny darling angels, waving and smiling, showering roses down from their pure white wings? Angels! thought Button. My baby is an angel now! It had never entered this sorrowful, disappointment-filled world but had lived safe within her body, loved and cherished, and then flown straight into God's heaven. Her face broke into a smile. Why, she, Button Bjork, was the mother of a real angel. Perhaps at night it winged its way down to sit on her bed and whisper words of comfort in her ear. Perhaps it said, "I love you, Mommie; don't be sad."

And for the first time the tears poured forth, cleansing her of all bitterness and spreading a balm over her bruised heart. After that she could laugh again. When Eric came home that night, she met him with a smile. The deep lines on his forehead disappeared as he smiled and took her in his arms.

"Eric," she whispered softly, "come with me into the nursery."

Silently he followed, holding her slender hand tightly in his strong one. In the doorway she stopped.

"Darling," she said, "do you know what? You and I are the parents of an angel, a tiny white-robed angel that can fly up and down between heaven and earth, and she will always love us, Eric, always. And someday this nursery will have other cribs and other babies will coo and smile and reach out little chubby arms toward us. But, dearest, no matter how many children God grants us, we'll never forget our first baby because she made a bridge for us to walk upon, a bridge covered with roses, that reaches all the way from earth to God's heaven."

CHAPTER 9

❧ Two Tiny Plants

Eric and Button waited four years for Charlene to join them and when she came, looking as beautiful as a tiny doll, their happiness knew no bounds. In another four years little Lynn arrived. Now they were really blessed.

"I am so glad there are four years between the girls," Button informed Vickey. "That way I was given enough time to get one little plant growing before I had to devote myself to the next one."

"Well, that's one way to look at it," laughed Vickey. "To tell you the truth, since I had to wait so many years for my first one, I was happy the other two followed closely."

"Probably I'm just finding an excuse for having had to wait so long between mine," confessed Button. "I felt it wasn't fair for me to have to wait so long when your three came one right after the other."

By now the nursery showed signs of having been well used, and the house echoed with laughter and singing. Button knew that God had been good to her. At times, she thought the wound in her heart had healed and that the memory of the angel had faded, but it was not so. When

151

she was alone, or when she awoke in the still of the night and couldn't go to sleep, the memories haunted her. Would God pass judgment on her for having carelessly killed her baby? Even if she hadn't meant to. . . . She should have listened to Eric begging her not to go out. In her mind she would again walk down that icy hill and feel herself falling, falling. . . . This introspection would leave her in a restless frame of mind and she would wonder if life could ever be the way it was before the accident?

Whenever this occurred, Button would seek out the girls wherever they were. If at night, she would tiptoe into their bedroom and stand beside their beds, listening to their even breathing and touching their golden curls. She would thank God over and over again that she had them. If during the day, she would leave her household tasks and walk with them to the park where they would feed the ducks and the long, shimmering goldfish. Engulfed in their childish chatter and happy laughter, her heart would find peace once again. Sometimes they would return late from these excursions, so after having fed and bathed the girls she would tuck them in their beds and listen to their prayers:

> "Bless our Daddy so kind and good
> And our Mommie who cooks our food.
> Bless the whole world that goes round and round
> And the birds that make such pretty sounds.
> Bless our mind, our soul, our heart,
> And let us not from Thee depart."

Button had written that prayer especially for her little girls. Often she occupied her mind by writing poems and prayers and sometimes an animal story to tell her daughters when they were good.

Early in the morning, right after Eric had left for work and while the girls were still in dreamland, Button would go out to work in her garden. She would kneel down on the soft grass and weed the flower beds. The world was beautiful in the early morning, so fresh and pure. The birds busy singing and building their nests and the sun shining lavishly down upon the earth would make Button's heart glad. How soft the dirt and how moist in her hands! The flowers bloomed these summers as never before, as if they wanted to show their thankfulness for the loving care they received. While she worked in the garden, no evil thoughts could penetrate her mind, but all was good and right and fine.

It had not taken Button long to discover that Charlene had inherited her mother's childish restlessness and naughtiness. At times she worried about her first-born daughter. She was too bright for her years, and her active mind could always find something to do—usually something she wasn't supposed to be doing. Many times the telephone would ring and there would be an irate voice at the other end of the line saying, "Mrs. Bjork, this is Mrs. Murphy, your neighbor three doors up the street. I want to inform you that the little girl of yours who looks like an angel with her blue eyes and golden curls—well, that little girl has just snipped off all my tulip blossoms—every single one of them and I had planned on using some of them for my centerpiece when I entertain the bridge club tomorrow night—and—and——"

"Mrs. Murphy," Button would hurry to say in order to stop the new complaint which she was certain would follow the first. "I'm so very sorry, but please forgive the little one. We often let her snip flowers in our garden, and she must have thought she could do it elsewhere. I'll have a bouquet sent to you from the florist; that is the only way I can compensate for her mistake."

And the next day:

"Is this you, Mrs. Bjork? Your little girl emptied my cream into the sandbox to make mudpies—my heavy cream, and I was having company today."

"Mrs. Jones! Thank you for calling me. I'm so sorry! I'm just on my way to the store, and I'll buy you another half-pint. I usually give Charlene the water for her mud-pies in a cream bottle so she must have been all mixed up. Please forgive her."

Button was at her wits' end with Charlene. And one day she had done far more than her share of mischief. There had been call after call complaining about her and several times she had ignored completely the things Button had asked her to do. Button decided that she was too leni-ent with this child, that was the whole story. Because she had lost her first baby, she was loving these two too much. But she would change her tactics. What Charlene needed was a good dose of the hairbrush, and this very night she would inflict a bit of Papa's discipline on the child.

"I must punish her," Button repeatedly told herself, paining at the thought.

The hairbrush might just be the thing to dispel Char-lene's naughtiness. She'd try it anyway, and she wouldn't spare that brush. Charlene would know that she had been punished.

Charlene had been bathed and powdered. Since she was a big girl now, she put herself to bed. It was time for

Button to tuck her in and read her a bedtime story. Lynn, a sweet baby who never fussed, had been asleep a long time.

She takes after her daddy, thought Button. She's as tranquil as a calm summer sea and loves harmonious and peaceful surroundings.

How thankful Button was for chubby, dimpled little Lynn and how she prayed that Charlene would outgrow her restlessness!

Button walked quickly up the stairs. The door was wide open. And surely the figure on the bed could be an angel, lying there so pink and soft in her dainty nightie. She stepped inside the door, hiding the instrument of punishment behind her back, but she had hardly got a foot inside the room when something flew at her as swiftly as an arrow and two soft arms wrapped themselves around her neck. A rosy cheek pressed against hers.

"Mommie," said a little voice in her ear, "Mommie, have I been a good girl today? I've tried so hard!"

The brush slipped to the floor. Button kissed Charlene tenderly, brushing her hand over the blonde curls.

"The best we can do is to try hard, darling," she whispered, a tear stealing down her cheek. "But tomorrow let's try a little harder."

She sat down on Charlene's bed and sang softly to her until her child's eyes were hidden behind the long dark lashes as if a priceless pair of drapes had been drawn closed. But Button remained seated on the bed for a long time, thinking and watching as sleep descended upon Charlene like a gentle benediction.

How could she have punished her? She was sure she had done the right thing, for when God looked into her own heart at night, perhaps He, too, had to smile as Button asked Him how well she had done. Could it be that she, too, deserved to be punished but that God, in His wisdom, judged her by how hard she had tried to do her best . . . how hard she had tried to be a good mother!

If ever there was a proud father, it was Eric! He played endlessly with the girls, bouncing them on his knees and spoiling them by bestowing upon them anything their hearts desired if it was within his means to do so. Never did he raise his voice to correct, nor his hand to punish them.

"It's all up to me," said Button grumpily, "all the unpleasant tasks of parenthood."

Very often quarrelsome words were exchanged between Eric and Button because of Charlene.

"You don't have to hit them to be a good parent," Eric protested. And always at times like that he would hide behind his newspaper and say no more, afraid that any further comments from him would throw his house into a state of confusion.

One day he came in unexpectedly and found Button whipping Charlene with a stick. She held the screaming child over her knee and energetically inflicted the paddling. Eric stood as if paralyzed.

"Button," he cried when he found his voice, "you that are so big ought to be ashamed to hit her that is so little!"

Button released Charlene and stared with hurt eyes at her husband. But the sharp remark she was about to make never left her lips. There was no use. Eric understood nothing when it came to rearing children. She gave him a desperate look which she hoped would penetrate deeper than words. What he needed to teach him a lesson was to stay home one whole day and watch Charlene. After that he, too, might be willing to use a stick on his offspring.

But later that night when, as always, Eric and Button discussed the issue, Eric had been considerate, kind and gentle.

"Button, perhaps you think I'm shirking my duty when it comes to disciplining the girls, but I have my own ideas of what is right. I was so often spanked as a small boy, I decided that, if I ever became a father, I'd never spank my children. You see, I want them always to keep the memory in their hearts that I was good to them."

Button drew a deep sigh.

"Well, dear, then I'm afraid they'll always remember me as an ogress of a mother, for someone has to punish them when they're naughty so that later in life they'll know how to discipline themselves . . . and with Charlene——"

"Quit being so critical of the child. She resents it, and it isn't good for you, either. Someday you'll end up a nervous wreck the way you carry on."

The sad thing was that Button had to admit that Eric was right. Charlene reminded her more and more of her own childhood and the naughty things she had done. Perhaps she resented this constant reminder and vented her feelings on her child. She didn't wish to recall the hurts she had inflicted upon Papa, for since Papa's death she wanted only the memory of their happy times together to remain in her mind.

So Button reverted to the way she had behaved in the parsonage . . . she withdrew from her dear ones. When they asked her to join their fun, she claimed a headache.

"What's wrong, dear?" Eric asked one night after the girls were tucked into bed. "You always complain of a headache these days and you're always tired. Don't you think you should see the new man who took Doctor Davis's place when he gave up his practice?"

"Oh, Eric, there's nothing wrong with me," Button assured him, forcing a laugh. "All mothers of young children get tired when night comes around."

Button knew that was not the truth. There was something vitally wrong. Sleep did not come quickly any more and she awoke unhappy in the morning.

Instead of a new doctor, I need Eric's arm around me, she thought, assuring me that I'm being a good mother. He makes me feel that I'm a failure and I want to be my very best!

Another thing that troubled Button was that she felt Eric had transferred all his affection to the girls. Before their arrival she had been the center of Eric's life, and now she had been pushed into a corner. Stronger and stronger this feeling grew within her—that lost, lonely feeling of not belonging to anyone.

Every Sunday afternoon Eric took the girls for a long walk. Button knew the little ones looked forward to this event all week. Lynn would ride in the stroller and Charlene would skip beside her. How dear they looked as they walked away! She longed to be part of that picture, but she had refused to accompany them so many times that they never invited her any more. All three seemed to be perfectly content to kiss her good-bye and be on their way.

They have a much better time without me, she thought sadly. Eric never gets cross with them. No wonder they love him so.

Perhaps she was too strict to compensate for his leniency; but who would discipline them if she didn't? Being parents carried certain responsibilities. Even that thought did not stop the pain in her heart.

Although she had consistently refused to join her little family in their outings, she dreaded being alone at home. Time and time again her thoughts went to the tiny baby she had never seen.

She would have been twelve this Christmas, she thought, and wondered what this child would have been like. Would she have had a restless nature such as Charlene's or would she had been serene and dimply like Lynn? Perhaps she would have differed from both of them. . . . Her heart longed for her dead baby until she shifted her thoughts to Papa, who never had seen her girls. Papa had passed away in Sweden the summer he and Mama had made a visit there. Mama had left him to sleep in Swedish soil, for she knew he had always wanted to rest in his homeland. It had been a dark day when the telegram from Sweden had reached America.

Mama had returned to America alone, and how beautifully Mama had mastered her sorrow! Button had been ashamed to manifest her grief for Mama's sake, so she pushed her great sorrow deep within her soul. It was only at times like this—although many years had passed—that she let herself grieve in loneliness for him.

"Papa, Papa, I miss you so," she whispered, her cheeks wet with tears. Life had never been the same without him. If only she could live those years with Papa over again, how differently she would live them.

Button knew that Papa had not been afraid to face death. She remembered that once, when they first had come to America, the whole family had taken a trip to Niagara Falls. She had been young then, but she had never forgotten Papa's words. He had held her arm as they had walked along in admiration and wonder over the mystery of God's creation, the magnificent beauty of the falls.

"Button," Papa had said as they stopped and listened to the mighty roar, "to me it seems that death must be like these falls. It comes roaring upon you with a tremendous force that nothing can stop. You are thrown and tossed and bruised and beaten upon the rocks, but suddenly you are swept into the stillness of the lake below and carried off into green pastures. Death is a tunnel between heaven and earth."

However, there were also days of sunshine and laughter. Button was her old self whenever the big Franzon family gathered on a Sunday night in one or another of the married children's homes. There were four of them married now. Vickey had been the first one. (It was she who had announced the glad news of the coming of the first grandchild when Mama returned from Sweden without Papa. Button had waited to tell her own news so as not to detract from Vickey's glowing pleasure.) Vickey had had her son before Button had had the "angel," and now Nim's Karin also was awaiting her first. Pelle and his wife, Felicia, were still studying, so for a while had postponed having a family. There were so many around the dinner table now that it was hard to find room for them all, but the place where Papa had sat remained empty, and it seemed odd they could be so gay without him.

Because of Eric's wish, Button refrained from using corporal punishment on Charlene again, but she had to find substitute ways by which to punish her when she had been extremely naughty. One trying day Button left her in the kitchen while she and Lynn went down the street to do some shopping. Her little human plants were growing up! And Charlene had to learn that being naughty did not pay. This particular day Charlene had gone to the extreme limit of naughtiness in whatever she had undertaken to do, so Button was going to teach her a lesson that she would not soon forget. It was a blazing hot July day and Button feared that perhaps she was punishing herself more by going than she was her daughter, but Charlene loved to go shopping and to deprive her of doing so might serve to make her more obedient in the future. Button put on a clean, crisp white summer dress and on Lynn she put a frilly pink one. Just the sight of the two of them all dressed up would set Charlene to thinking, she hoped.

"Charlene," she said, taking her daughter's small tanned hand in hers, "I'm doing this to teach you a lesson. I hope Lynn and I will never need to go without you again. Do you understand this?"

Charlene nodded her head, looking up at Button with large innocent blue eyes that always tempted Button to take her in her arms and hug her to her heart, but she refrained.

"Mommie, why am I naughty?" she asked.

"I wish I knew, Charlene. You really have a heart of gold, but you do all the wrong things that make the neighbors complain about you. For instance, why did you cut the rope by which Duberry's new pup was tied? It allowed him to run away, and they spent hours looking for him."

"But God sent him back when I prayed that I was sorry."

"Yes, but see what extra work you made for God!"

"I never thought of that. Next time I won't bother Him."

"Oh, Charlene, Charlene darling, perhaps Mommie said the wrong thing. I don't think God minded. He is so good and He loves you so. But now, I want you to stay in the kitchen and not leave it until we get back. You may sit by the table and draw pictures. And while you're sitting there, you might think of one good deed you can do—a very unusual deed—something no one else would bother to do. This will show Mommie that you want to be a good girl."

"I will, Mommie! I know I'll think of something and next time I'll go with you and Lynn when you shop. Won't I?"

"I hope so, darling!"

But even while shopping, Button couldn't help but long for Charlene. How she missed that child. Perhaps she had punished her foolishly this time. She might not even stay in the kitchen but go out into the neighborhood and devise more mischief. The thought was alarming and caused Button to stop shopping sooner than she had anticipated. She hurried home but found Charlene seated at the table drawing pictures and being as good as could be. This, then, must have been the right punishment in spite of her qualms. Button clasped Charlene in her arms, relieved that the episode was over. Charlene wasn't mean, just naughty, and she would outgrow it. Some plants needed special care and Charlene was one of those rare stubborn ones, but once they started to grow they proved to be the most beautiful flowers of all.

It wasn't until suppertime that Button noticed the spots on the ceiling. She called Eric's attention to them.

"Look, Eric, there must be a leak in the upstairs bathroom. You'd better look into it right away."

"I can't see a thing wrong," said the puzzled Eric after he had checked the bathroom. "The floor, however, looks as if it had been all wet and then wiped up. . . . Charlene," he said, "do you happen to know anything of water running in the bathroom?"

Charlene nodded. "It did overflow, but he wiped it all up. The rags are down the cellar."

"He?" asked Eric and Button simultaneously. "Who is he?"

"Oh, the garbage man, of course!"

"The garbage man! Please, please, Charlene, tell us quickly what the garbage man was doing in our bathroom?"

"That's a secret," smiled Charlene, "a great big secret between God and me!"

"But Mommie and I want to know, honey," said Eric and took the child in his lap. "You'll tell Daddy, won't you?"

"Is the deed just as good if I talk about it? Will it make me just as un-naughty?"

"Yes, yes, darling!" Button's heart was beating like a sledge hammer by now.

"I saw Mr. Garbage Man sitting in the yard eating a sandwich. He looked terribly hot and dirty and, Mommie, you asked me to think of a deed that no one else would do— so I called to him and asked if he wanted to take a shower to cool off and get all clean. He was up there a long time and after he was gone the ceiling was wet, so when I saw the water, I made him come back and wipe it all up. He was a very nice garbage man and so good. He even said thank you and patted me on the head. He said I was the nicest girl he had ever seen and that my folks should thank God for having me. Wasn't that a real honest-to-goodness good deed, Mommie?"

Button and Eric looked at each other, his look accusing her, and hers pleading with him to understand why she had punished Charlene by leaving her alone. With each other they only conversed with their eyes, but to Charlene they reached out their arms.

"We'll talk about it some other time, honey, but you did a very unusual deed, indeed, and we know you meant it from your heart," smiled Button. "I don't believe that man will ever forget you."

Those years the Bjorks spent their summer vacations in the White Mountains since now they could rent the whole cabin where they had spent their honeymoon. What fun and enjoyment they had during these two weeks. They took advantage of every moment, spending their time boating, swimming, fishing and hiking through the woods.

One evening Eric had gone fishing, and Button and the two girls had sat on the dock and watched him row away. The gentle night was creeping in upon them. The stars would soon twinkle over the woodland. A whippoorwill called from a tall treetop, and a big round moon was beginning to peek from behind the mountains. To think that here it was they had spent their honeymoon. Isn't life wonderful, thought Button, holding an arm around each of the girls. God was good to have given her these tender plants to nurture, and it seemed as if Charlene was at last overcoming her bad traits; she had been as good as gold for a long time.

Their nearest neighbors, the Goldbergs, were packing their station wagon in order to leave in the early morning hours. They had just been over to say good-bye. They were from Philadelphia and the two families had become good friends. Button was happy that her own vacation still had a week to go, for, although she would miss their neighbors, to be completely alone with Eric and the girls would be like a little bit of heaven—a whole long week.

"Mommie, what is a honeymoon?" asked Lynn. "Is that one coming up behind the mountains?"

"No, darling, a honeymoon is when two people go away someplace and no one knows where they are. They just whisper sweet words to each other and are so nice that the whole world seems sweet like golden honey."

"Is that why Daddy and you are always nice?" asked Charlene.

"Perhaps so, dear. Daddy and I had a wonderful honeymoon, as you know, right here in this log cabin, and no one in the whole world knew we were here."

Button put the girls to bed, hoping that her definition of a honeymoon would suffice. After all, how could she explain the meaning of honeymoon to two little girls?

The children slept in the back room in a big double bed, pleased and proud to be bunking together. Now that Lynn was getting older, Charlene and she had more things in common and they seemed content in each other's company. That might be the reason for Charlene's better behavior.

The following morning Eric and Button slept later than usual. That was one of the satisfying things about a vacation, that there were no time schedules to keep, no rushing about, just complete relaxation. Button awoke in a happy mood. She would surprise her family and make *plättar* for breakfast. They all loved these tiny, flat Swedish pancakes, and she had real lingonberries to serve with them. She worked quietly so as not to awaken the others until everything was ready. She set the table on the porch, overlooking the lake and flooded with bright sunshine. All being done to perfection, she went to call the girls. It was most unusual to have them sleep so late, yet she had not heard a sound from their room.

Button pushed the door open quietly and then her heart stopped.

"Eric," she screamed, "they are gone—the girls are not in their beds!"

She had never seen Eric fly so fast. He searched every nook and cranny, inside and out.

"They must be playing a game and hiding somewhere." He tried to sooth Button, but she could sense that he, too, believed that something more serious had happened.

After a long, futile search the village police were called, and they combed the woods and searched in all the empty cottages. With nothing to do but wait, the endless hours seeming long as weeks. Could the children have been kidnaped? Button refused to believe so, for who would take two little girls whose parents were not wealthy?

At three o'clock in the afternoon, emotionally exhausted, Eric and Button were sitting on the porch, trying to comfort each other when the Goldbergs' station wagon drove into the yard.

"Look, Eric," exclaimed Button, "the Goldbergs must have heard about the girls and they have come back to help us. . . . How can we ever be thankful enough to God for friends like that . . . ?" But she had time to say no more before the two girls flew out of the car and into their arms. They were hugged and kissed and squeezed while tears ran down both Eric's and Button's cheeks. Mr. Goldberg stood beside them, but his face was not radiant. His wife remained in the car. Finally Eric found his voice.

"But—but—how does it happen you are with the Goldbergs?"

"Yes—how? I may be fired from my job for not showing up on time," fretted Mr. Goldberg. "And my wife gets motion sick, and now we have all this extra distance to go. We had gone many miles before we discovered them. They had crawled under the seats in the back and had fallen asleep on an old blanket. With the suitcases piled high on the seats, we never knew they were there until we heard Lynn whimper that she wanted to go home."

"But why—why did you get into the wagon?"

"We went on a honeymoon to be good," sobbed Lynn. "Charlene said to."

"Mommie, you said if two went away alone and no one knew about it, the whole world would be sweet like honey. Lynn and I wanted to try it. Was it naughty?" asked Charlene.

Even the Goldbergs couldn't help joining in the laughter.

"Let that be a lesson to you," said Mr. Goldberg. "Next time you talk about your honeymoon, be sure the girls aren't around. You never know what ideas pop into children's heads. It was lucky they just went into our station wagon."

That night Eric and Button thanked God that their family was together again. Those had been anxious hours without Charlene and Lynn, but they had not been scolded for their impromptu trip. This was all part of growing up. Soon they would be tiny plants no longer but would have to guide their own lives . . . and those few hours they had been lost had been like death itself.

"Oh," said Eric, "in the excitement I forgot to notify the police. Everyone has been so kind to us, but this will be the happiest news I've ever carried."

And never had two parents been so thankful.

BOOK III

CHAPTER 10

❧ Years That Trembled

I am going for a walk, Eric," called Button from the front hall, as she put on her jacket and tied a bandana around her hair.

"I wish I could go with you," answered Eric from upstairs. He was reading a bedtime story to Lynn. "But someone has to stay with the girls."

Button walked out into the dusk of an autumn evening which was permeated with the pungent smell of burning leaves. She chose the road leading through the park. A bit of blushing sky was still visible where the sun had descended to the horizon, but Button was blind to the beauty around her. Nor did she smell the smoking leaves. She was hardly aware of the season of the year, having but one purpose in mind, to walk as fast as her feet would carry her. If she had been much younger, she would have run swiftly down the street, through the park, up the hill and down again. A woman in her forties, however, does not run, nor does she cry or laugh or scream or give vent to any emotion in public as she walks along. She simply places one foot before the other and holds her head high. If she

171

meets an acquaintance, she nods and forces a smile to her lips, even though her heart may be breaking.

As Button walked along, she tried not to think of the past years, and she tried not to think of the years ahead. She had to live in the present, a fact which she had never faced before. She had to put an end to her dreaming and learn to be like other people because she was sure that was the way Eric wanted her to be.

"No one can say that I haven't been a good mother," she told herself. "No one can say that I haven't tried to make my marriage a success. And Eric and I have been as happy as two people can be . . . we've shared whatever life has brought our way . . . we've loved our home and planted and cared for our garden . . . we've loved our girls and have given them not only material things but lofty thoughts, as well, that would feed their souls. Long ago we sorrowed over our first-born, whom we never held in our arms. When Papa left this earthly life, and I grieved for his going, Eric stood close beside me, a bulwark of strength and comfort. We have done all we could to create happiness, but inside my heart there's a vast emptiness, a crying, a knocking. I hear it at night when I sleep; I feel it the first thing in the morning when I open my eyes. I can't get away from it. I can't tell Eric about it, for he wouldn't understand. I don't know what to do . . . I just don't know."

She walked fast as she thought. Walking helped a little when she could walk alone. It was as though she wanted to escape from the gloom that entrapped her, but it was always waiting for her inside the door of her own home when she returned. She had felt like this for the past few years and she was not getting better. Where she was head-ing she did not know and she was afraid to face the future. What had happened to her? Somewhere, back in the years, she had lost herself. Part of her was still crying and calling her back. But life's highway is a one-way street and one cannot turn back. Once she had been gay and full of laughter. Now there was only sadness. Once she had dreamed beautiful dreams. Now she had lost the magic and the daring of dreaming. How does one who is broken to pieces become whole again? Once she had walked and talked with God, and she had given Him her special dream to keep in His care, believing that someday He would give it back to her, but He had not. How noble had been her dreams of becoming an author and writing a book that would make people laugh! She knew now that she would never write. Her head ached constantly from too much thinking, and the tension within her increased with each new day. She somehow had lost the real Button . . . but worse than that, she had lost her God, and there was no tragedy worse than that. And there was no Papa to talk to or to advise her.

For years after she was married she talked about dreams. She told Eric, "You must learn to dream," but Eric had been cross with her.

"That's the trouble with you, Button. You don't live in a real world. You're always up in the clouds. Fantasy is forgivable in one who is young, but you're not a child, you're a mature woman. Now you must act like one. What will the girls think? Don't you suppose they want a mother who acts like other mothers? The mothers of the children they know talk about how to make dresses and how to fix their hair and of the latest party and who is invited and who is not. They talk of school doings and the P.T.A. and many other everyday things. But our children's mother

talks about writing books and flying to the moon and picking money from the street."

That was the longest speech Button had ever heard
Eric make. She had stood there hurt and ashamed. She
had had no idea that those were his sentiments.

"I'll try hard, Eric, to be different," she said meekly.
"I'll do my best not to dream, but you knew I was like that
when you married me. If you had just wanted an ordinary,
sane woman, you should never have married me."

"Now dear," uttered Eric apologetically as he placed
his arm around her, "I didn't mean to hurt you. You were
all right for me and I didn't mind that talk, though I never
understood it, but we have two daughters now. Please, Button, try to understand what I am trying to tell you without
getting your feelings hurt."

She honestly tried, but the hurt grew deeper each day
and her head ached more and more. One day Eric suggested taking her to the doctor. Button hesitated about going, for she felt that no new doctor could ever take kind old
Dr. Davis's place, but reluctantly she went and found that
Dr. Hasselton was very pleasant and just as kind as their old
doctor had been. He gave her a very thorough physical
examination and then spoke to Eric, who was waiting in the
outer office.

"Mr. Bjork, there seems to be no physical cause for
your wife's troubles. I would say the trouble lay more in an
emotional conflict. Her nerves are not very steady. There
seems to be something depressing her, making her moody
like a person without hope. Can you give any reason for
this?"

But Eric knew none.

The doctor shook his head. "It's hard to prescribe a

remedy when one doesn't know the cause of a condition. All I can suggest for the time being is that you give your wife a good time, make her laugh, have fun so she will find life enjoyable. This is very important, so do your best, for if she remains in this state, I'm afraid that she is headed for a serious nervous breakdown."

After that visit, Eric became so considerate and thoughtful that it was almost unbearable to Button. He endeavored to anticipate her every wish and kept the girls from tiring her whenever he was near.

"Remember, Charlene, Mommie isn't well; no noise, please."

And to Lynn, "Don't bother Mommie when Daddy is here. We must be very careful with her, remember?"

Thus, whenever she entered a room where the girls were, they dropped whatever they were doing and walked on tiptoe, looking at her wistfully as if she were a person from another planet. This was the last thing Button wanted, to be estranged from her daughters, but how could they understand what was even beyond her own knowledge?

Button missed Mama, too. She had moved to sunny Florida where, Nim had informed her, her life span would be increased immeasurably. Nim and Karin lived in Florida also. Nim was a surgeon now, "and a very busy one," Mama wrote. Mama did not live with her son and his wife. She had sold her Northern home and had bought a brand-new cottage in Miami. She was very happy there, and she still had Kerstin with her. Both Torkel and Calle were in theological school studying for the ministry, following in Papa's footsteps. Pelle and Felicia were still in the East, as was Greta, who was teaching school. It was strange to think that the large Franzon family were all scattered now, close as they had been while Papa was still with them and they lived in the parsonage. Button remembered that once long ago in Lapland, Papa had told them that this was bound to happen.

"We must be thankful as long as we can all be together," he had said one day after the morning prayer. "Life will part us soon enough when you all grow up and get married and have your own homes. It's wonderful to be as close to each other as we now are, but the years will change that and we will grow apart. Life has a way of running out of time very quickly."

The next day, when it was Nim's turn to pray, he had ended with these words, "Thank you, God, that we can all be so happy together in our parsonage. Please don't let us part from each other, but let us all die together."

Button missed Mama's daily telephone calls most of all. Each morning Mama used to call her and she always sounded happy as a lark. Those calls had made each day begin a little brighter for Button.

"Hello, Button," she would say. "What a wonderful new day God has given us to be glad in."

And then they had talked of everyday things, and Mama in her sunny way had solved any problems that troubled Button. Now Mama was hundreds of miles away and Papa still farther.

That night, when Button returned from her walk, Eric was waiting by the door. He took her jacket and hung it in the closet.

"You were gone a long, long time. I was worried about you," he said kindly.

"Oh, I'm sorry, Eric. I was just walking. Somehow, I

feel better when I walk, but now I'm very tired and, if you don't mind, I'll go right to bed."

She was undressed and in bed in a few moments. Eric brought her a cup of hot milk.

"Drink this and you'll feel much better. I hope you'll sleep through the whole night," he said as he sat down on the edge of the bed.

Exhausted as she was, sleep would not come. Hours later when Eric came to bed, she pretended to be asleep, lying very still with her eyes closed. It wasn't long before Eric's heavy breathing told her he was asleep. She opened her eyes wide then and stared at a small patch of light reflected on the ceiling from the streetlight. She knew she would lie awake for hours and hours, and the night would be dreadfully long. Toward morning she might doze for a short while but awaken at the slightest noise, exhausted from the lack of sleep. It had been like that night after night for a long time; for how long, she had stopped trying to recall.

There were sleeping tablets in the medicine cabinet and, if the night became too unbearable, she would take one. . . . Sleep finally came but not a restful sleep.

The next day her nerves were even more tense and her gloom thicker. Somehow she must get hold of herself, recapture the gay spirit of her former years. There must be something that could mend those nerves!

One day when she came home from her walk, Mama was there. What a happy surprise! Eric had written asking Mama to come, and she planned to spend a whole month with them. Button could relax from all responsibility, for Mama took over the household. Happiness reigned for a short while, but soon Button drifted back to her moodiness, and there was nothing Mama could do to help her.

"Well, I've done all I can," exclaimed Eric, throwing up his hands in despair. "I don't know what more I can do."

"We have to wait—and pray, Eric," soothed Mama. "Pray that God will make her well. And don't despair or lose courage. It's all for a purpose, for in God's plan He takes even the bad and turns it to the good. Only, we must have patience."

"But it has been such a long time since she was well. Perhaps she never will be cured at home. A rest home might be the answer, Mama? If she got away from us all, she might get well much faster."

"Well, let's wait a little longer," said Mama. "Nerves take a long time to heal; we all know that."

And Eric waited. Mama went back to her sunshine, and Button escaped further and further from them all into a world of her own—a strange, dark, fearful world.

One sleepless night while Button lay staring at the ceiling, a wild desire came over her to go for a drive. She slipped softly from the bed so as not to awaken Eric and made her way to the garage. Soon she was driving along the highway with the dark night enveloping her. It had been a daring thing to do, and Eric certainly would not have approved if he knew about it. Yet, if she drove fast, she left that gnawing feeling at the pit of her stomach behind her. She drove thus for two hours and then returned to the house. All was still. Eric was a sound sleeper and did not waken when she crept into bed beside him. She felt better than she had felt in months and soon fell into a deep untroubled sleep.

This drive in the dead of night gave her something to

hold on to. Faster and faster she had driven on the highway, farther and farther from the city, until at last calmness descended on her disturbed spirit. Then she had turned toward home. As she drove along, she had tried to find an anchor that would hold her fast. She reached out desperately for whatever she thought would help. The thought of God came first, the friendly God she had known in her youth, the God who had lived with the Franzons in the parsonage. Button remembered how secure they all felt when Papa and Mama went calling and left them alone because the last thing Mama would say was, "You be good children now. Know that God is right here with you while we're away. He will watch over you carefully, but remember, you can't put anything over on Him. If you're good, we might bring something nice home with us. Who knows?"

After Mama and Papa had left, Button recalled, they had wondered where God was sitting.

"Perhaps on the sofa," Calle had suggested. "There's no other place big enough."

They all had agreed that Calle was right and they had walked around the sofa very carefully, wondering what God would look like if they could see Him. When, by chance, a storm came up while Papa and Mama were gone, and the thunder rolled ominously and the lightning flashed threateningly, they had not been afraid, for who could fear with God himself keeping guard over them!

"I believe that is God out riding," Greta had said, as she pressed her face against the window and watched the rain pouring down in torrents. "And when we see the lightning, it's the fire from the wheels of God's chariot, for His horses run so fast that, when the wheels go over the stars, it looks like fire."

Yes, although their parsonage God had been very strict and despised sin, He had also been very good and watchful; it was comforting to have a God such as that. Now she had almost completely lost Him. But she must and she would hold on to herself so she would overcome her inner disturbances and once more be well again. She recalled a story from the Bible of Jacob's wrestling with God; maybe she, too, would have to wrestle with God before she could again find peace and be cured of every ill.

The third time Button took the car at night, Eric was waiting for her when she came home. He had a light on in the living room, and she could see him pacing back and forth. She stood in the doorway, her eyes looking pleadingly into his. He must understand that this driving was something she was compelled to do by a force within her that was stronger than herself.

"Button," said Eric kindly, "sit down on the sofa and we'll have a little talk."

Automatically she sat down.

"You know," he said, taking her hand in his, "this can't go on any longer. Can't you imagine how worried I was to know that you were out in the middle of the night, driving who knows where in your tired state of mind? Please, promise me that you won't take the car out any more at night."

"No, Eric, please don't make me promise that because driving at night has really helped me. After I come back, I can sleep."

"For my sake, dear, please!"

"No, I can't. It helps me, and I'll get well soon."

"Then there is no other course that I can take. . . . I'll take you to Doctor Hasselton tomorrow afternoon, and

he'll have to make arrangements to place you in a rest
home. It will be a private place, my dear, but a place where
you can get well."

Button stared at Eric for a long time. Then her eyes
filled with tears.

"Eric, I haven't lost my mind, if that's what you're
thinking. But if you send me away, I am sure I will. Driving the car at night has helped me. I can sleep when I come
home, and my heart does not beat so rapidly. Please, Eric,
just let me drive, and I promise I'll soon be well."

But Eric would not. After that the door to the garage
was locked, and Eric kept the key on his key ring. Button
had never been so frightened. Wasn't there anyone who
could help her? She hadn't lost her reason; she was only
sick. . . . What would she do if Eric put her in—in that
place?

One day Eric took her again to Doctor Hasselton.
While she was dressing in the examination room, Eric and
the doctor conferred in the adjoining office. She pressed
close against the wall and tried to listen to their conversation.

"I can't take it any longer, Doctor," Eric pleaded.
"You'll have to help us."

Doctor Hasselton answered very softly. Button
strained her ears to hear him but could not, so she dressed
very quickly and joined them in the office, looking anxiously from one to the other.

The doctor shook Eric's hand and, patting Button on
the shoulder, said, "Be a good girl now, Button. We'll soon
have you sitting on top of the world. I'll see you in a week,
and I hope to have a very good report from Eric concerning
you."

She wondered about that as they drove home. Did Doctor Hasselton mean that she would get better in a private rest home where people were confined who had lost their minds, or did he mean that he had persuaded Eric that she was better off at home? One thing she knew, that Eric could not confine her without a doctor's signature. The next time she saw him, she would ask him, but not Eric. She would try to act well . . . she would pretend to sleep . . . she would pretend that she was happy . . . she would be a good actress. Perhaps if she earnestly tried, God would help her . . . at least she would ask Him.

Button tried very hard to act as if she felt well, but it didn't fool Eric. Some people claim love is blind, but that certainly wasn't true with Eric, whose love made him see more sharply. He couldn't read Button's thoughts, so he believed this behavior to be a new phase of her illness. The lines in his face deepened, and his eyes looked sadder each day. There seemed to be nothing Button could do to help him, for her heart couldn't ache any longer . . . it felt dull and heavy, and she didn't care what either Eric or the girls were thinking. She felt as though she lived in another world. The years were trembling beneath her feet; there was nothing she could hold on to. If only Papa had been with her. Papa would have understood, for he knew everything; he would have found a way for her to get well. He would have said, "You're not giving up, are you, Button?" She could hear his voice, so full of strength and assurance. "Our life is like a ship. If we have an able captain, we will never lose our course."

Those words he had spoken long ago, and she wished she could hear him say them again. Then she remembered herself—the former Button—the one she had lost back in the years . . . the Button she had been before she lost her angel and before Papa left this earth. . . . That Button had been strong. Then she heard a voice within her, reminding her of the promise she had made to herself that, even though life's storms made her bend very low, she would never, never break. Something stirred within her— a longing—a caring for life that had been absent for too long a time. She heard herself speak:

"I must will myself to be better. I must believe that tomorrow is better than yesterday . . . I must will to will . . . will to will . . ." And somehow, from that moment, she found the incentive to try to get well.

"Father God," she prayed that night, "give me back my faith in life, in my loved ones, in my dream—and in You."

As night closed around her, there was hope in her for the first time since her illness, as though a star had pierced her darkness to let God's light shine through to her soul.

CHAPTER 11

❧ Dear Doctor

Button had an appointment with Doctor Hasselton. She had come to his office half an hour early. It was pleasant to sit in his lovely waiting room and somehow, here, it didn't hurt her to think. It was strange how close she had grown to feel toward this new doctor. It was almost as if Doctor Davis had never been, and yet he had been the Franzon family doctor and friend from the time they had come from Sweden until his retirement. He and his gentle wife had moved to California, and at first the world had seemed empty without him. Not that there had been much sickness in the parsonage, for Mama had prayed most of it away! But there had been many talks over the telephone and an endless amount of advice from the kind doctor, who felt that for the best welfare of the community a doctor and minister should work closely together. Button wished Doctor and Mrs. Davis a most enjoyable sunset of life as they lived its last chapter.

It was Doctor Davis who had recommended Doctor Hasselton to Eric when he had written him, asking his advice concerning Button's illness. Doctor Davis had given his successor the finest recommendation:

184

Doctor Hasselton is a fine medical doctor, advisor and surgeon. He is also very cognizant of the fact that emotional disturbances can cause physical suffering. He is a fine church member, which would be important to Button. I have complete confidence in his ability and believe that he can cope with any situation. If anyone can help our Button, Doctor Hasselton can.

That had been five years ago . . . a long five years during which Button had been ill, not with a disease that could be easily diagnosed, such as of the liver or heart, but one that couldn't be pinpointed. That it was nerves, both the doctor and family agreed, but what caused them to act in this behavior pattern was something not easily answered.

Well, Button thought, if everything could be just black or white or rosy colored . . . but into the tapestry of life must also be woven the grays and they were the nonunderstandable ones. Beautiful blues and greens were fine, blended with golden colors from blushing sunsets and majestic sunrises, for they signified life at its best. White stood for a heart right with God, black for life's sorrow, but gray represented turmoil and confusion—dull, dreary, monotonous gray being painfully woven into the fabric of her life.

Button was glad that Doctor Hasselton was such a fine man, easy to talk to and easy to look at. He must be about her own age, she reflected, with dark hair and brown eyes that penetrated deeply as he consulted with his patients. Button liked his hands best—strong and firm but gentle hands from which strength seemed to flow as he placed them on hers when she was troubled. Sometimes with his hand on hers, she felt as if she had been given a transfusion of new life. No matter how dark the shadows were around her, after a talk with the doctor, they lightened.

Today she had an important question to ask the doctor.

He came into the office earlier than usual and his kind nurse opened the door of the waiting room.

"Doctor Hasselton is ready for you now, Mrs. Bjork," she beckoned smilingly.

A few minutes later Button was sitting in a comfortable chair opposite his desk. He smiled across at her and she returned his smile timidly. Strange how much easier it was to smile at the doctor than at Eric.

He began the conversation. "You're looking very well today, Button. I hope you'll tell me that you feel as well as you look?"

"I wish I could, Doctor. Whenever I'm here with you, I feel fine. All my fears and troubles disappear. I think each time I leave your office that the coming week will be a good one in which I'll make great progress, but the minute I close your door all my fears return."

"There's no need to give you a physical exam each time you come in, Button, nor to take your blood pressure, so we'll spend our time just talking. In spite of everything you say, I'm going to make believe that you really are better. Will you co-operate and help me in my game?"

"I'll try!"

"Eric phoned me last night. We had a long talk, and he expects much from your visit with me today."

"Too much, perhaps! Please tell me, is he planning to send me to an asylum?"

"What a terrible way to put it, Button. Certainly not an asylum. Eric has a rest home in mind, a place where a person like you can get the care and rest that you need and come out cured. Those places are very expensive, and it will take all your savings if you go. Don't think that Eric would even consider a place like that except in your best interest. Believe me, Button, he's tried his best all these years to help you, but you don't respond very well."

"I know. I'm sorry for him, for me, for the girls. I know Eric has the best in mind, but I will not go—not even to a home like that. . . . Please, Doctor Hasselton, help me." And Button gazed at the doctor with wide imploring eyes, full of helplessness and despair.

The office was very still. The telephone rang and the doctor talked with another patient. Button's eyes wandered around the room and suddenly the odor of antiseptics and the sight of the prescription pad made her feel fenced in. She had a wild impulse to run, just to get away, but the next moment she was composed again.

"Button," said Doctor Hasselton very gently, "I want to help you! But if I persuade Eric not to send you to a home, you must work with me. You see, neither I nor anyone else can mend your frayed nerves. You're the only one who can do it. It's up to you, so let's try a little longer and harder to get at the root of your trouble. There's something buried, deep, deep within you, that is the cause of your illness. It's bottled up there and if we don't release it, you'll be blown to pieces as if by an explosion. Will you search deep and try to tell me what it is?"

"I'll try. You know, I lost my first baby. I fell on the ice and it died. I killed it."

"You know better. You loved that baby and wanted it more than life itself. You did *not* kill it any more than I kill a person upon whom I am called to operate too late."

"Thank you. I'll try to think of it in that light. I don't dwell on it too often now. I'm too tired."

"That could have been the beginning of your trouble, the shock to your nerves, but you're much too intelligent to let that incident alone ruin your health."

"It's missing Papa, too! Sometimes I think I can't stand to live without Papa. I grieve over the heartaches I caused him when I was little. . . . I—I . . ."

Button placed her head on the desk and let her tears flow. Doctor Hasselton lifted up her face and shook his head. He wiped the tears from her eyes.

"You're not a little girl any more, Button, but a grown woman. You know that we all have to part with our loved ones. Your father was an old man and ready to enter into the larger life. Would you be selfish enough to hold him back from what God had prepared for him? We who have hope in this mystery called immortality do not sorrow as do those without hope of eternal life. You still have your mother. I lost both my parents when I was young, and believe me, my dear, I loved them dearly and life was hard to face without them. But do you think I should have given up my talent and sacrificed my career to devote my time to grieving? Would that have brought them back?"

"Oh, no, I can see how selfish I've been. I was only thinking of my own loss!"

Button tried to force a smile, but it soon died on her lips.

"Doctor, do you think I could have married the wrong man? Perhaps I don't love Eric the way I should?"

Doctor Hasselton laughed a hearty laugh.

"Forgive me, Button, but your question struck me funny. You see, in my profession I see so much of the inside of people's marriages. I recognize an unhappy marriage when I see one, but from what I have seen of you and Eric, I'd say you were made for each other. Think of how he has stood by you and loved you and been concerned over you through all these years of your sickness. That takes real love, believe me, for he's had to live through many dark hours. Yet all he wants is for you to get well . . . not only for his sake but more for your own. He wants you to live again in your world of joy that was such an integral part of you. He told me that you used to be so gay no one could come near you without catching a good share of it."

"I know you must be right, but being so confused that question just popped into my head. I know if I were well, Eric and I would be very happy together. Perhaps it is Charlene. I may get too upset with worry over that child. She's constantly doing things she shouldn't do."

"Now you are looking for a needle in a haystack. If all parents of naughty children became as ill as you are, we would have a pretty sick world! Often, you know, the naughtiest children grow up to be the smartest people. The alertness and inventiveness that cause so much mischief when they're young become their most admirable traits when they mature. You have two lovely daughters, Button, and neither one of them could be the cause for your breakdown."

There was one more thing. It flickered like a light within her heart. It was her dream—her writing—but somehow she couldn't talk about it. . . . There was no use to try. . . . He might laugh at her, thinking she was just trying to find things for him to analyze.

"I suppose, I should be ashamed of myself," she said, "for when it comes right down to it, I don't have any reason for my trouble. But it's there. . . . I can't get rid of it . . . it grows and grows. . . . I don't know what to do."

Doctor Hasselton stood up. "Well, my dear," he smiled, "you've done your best for today. We'll find this thing that troubles you. Now promise me that you won't worry over the cause of your illness. From now on you let me worry about that! And you can feel assured that no one, not even Eric, can send you away without my consent. I am your doctor, Button, and you must trust me. I'll do everything in my power to help you. I won't let you down, I promise."

She shook his hand. "I don't know how to express what I feel, but I am so very grateful. I feel as if a heavy burden had been lifted from me. I feel confident that, as long as you stand by me, we can lick this thing together. I, too, promise not to let you down."

He put his arm around her shoulder and smiled down on her. "I like to hear you say that, Button. You wait and see; this may be the end of all your confusion. I feel that today we have really accomplished something worth while."

Button walked home feeling happier than she had in years. Oh, Doctor Hasselton was the most wonderful man she had ever known. He would never, never let anyone send her away from her home—not even Eric!

That night, when she returned from her long walk, she felt happy. Eric was working in the cellar, fixing a bicycle for Lynn. The girls were asleep. The house was still and peaceful. Button sat down at her Governor Winthrop desk in the cozy living room and almost before she realized it, she had started a letter:

Dear Doctor,

I must write to you tonight. During every minute
of my long walk, my thoughts were with you in your
office. I could see your face as kindly and patiently
you minister to those who come to seek your help. You
are so wonderfully kind, and I want you to know that
my heart is so full of gratitude that I can hardly express it. You are the most wonderful person I have ever
met. Thank you for giving life back to me anew. I can
live it now without fear. I shall get well because of
you. Nothing in the whole world can harm me. I shall
go to bed after I have mailed this letter, and I believe
that I will fall asleep quickly. I hope that you understand what I am trying to say. Words seem so inade-
quate to express what is in my heart. Please realize
that those long hours you give to mankind are worth
while . . . so very worth while.

Good night,
Button

She hurried to the corner to mail her letter before
Eric came up from the cellar. When he did, Button was
sitting in her favorite blue chair, reading a magazine.

"Button," he said, with beaming face, "how well you
look tonight and so happy. It's good to see you sitting there
just like old times."

"I feel better, Eric, a lot better. I hope it continues."

That night she was awakened only once by her own
thoughts, which were again with Doctor Hasselton. She
hoped that he had a kind and understanding wife, for tomorrow he might have to mend another broken heart. Soon
she drifted back to sleep, a happy smile playing on her lips.

Button did not walk alone any more. Doctor Hasselton

walked beside her. They did not speak to each other, but he was there; a dream figure, of course, but more real than flesh and blood to Button. She felt secure now. Life had meaning once more. At last she had found something to hold on to, and the old sparkle began to return to her eyes.

It was time for another visit. Wouldn't Doctor Hasselton be surprised! He wouldn't recognize her as the same person. Going to his office was as much fun as going on a trip.

As she sat in the waiting room, an unexpected fear came over her. She hadn't given it a thought before, but had she been foolish to write him, busy as he was? She could not even remember what she had written. She should not have mailed her letter so soon before thinking over what she had said. Anxiety filled her. Perhaps Doctor Hasselton would scold her in a polite way and tell her he was a very busy man . . . that he had to limit his time with each patient to the office visit . . . that reading letters was not expected of him as a medical doctor. . . . Oh, why had she done such a foolish thing! She always rushed into things impulsively, without thinking, and now this last might be worse than the first. Button almost decided to walk out of the waiting room, make an excuse to the nurse, when . . .

"Your turn, Mrs. Bjork!" said the nurse from the doorway, and there, inside the other door, she could see Doctor Hasselton's smiling face.

"Why, Button!" he exclaimed. "You look wonderful today. I was so happy your shared your thoughts with me. Do you still sleep well?"

"Doctor Hasselton, I want to apologize for bothering you with my letter. . . . I'm so ashamed of myself. I just didn't stop to think. You see, the minute I sat down to write, the whole world straightened out for me. I forgot that you are a busy doctor and can't be expected to spend your valuable time reading silly letters——"

"Button, what are you saying? Now stop that kind of talk this moment. Anything that helps to soothe your nerves is a tonic for you and all right with me. My time is consecrated to helping my patients, and it doesn't matter to me whether it is through office visits or reading letters. My only concern is to cure my patients."

"Thank you, that is a great relief. . . . I was so worried!"

After the examination and the usual preliminaries were over, Doctor Hasselton handed Button a prescription.

"Button," he said, "don't take this to the druggist. Because of its importance, I have written it out for you. It is not a prescription for a new tonic or stronger sleeping pills, but I believe it will work better."

Button glanced down at the paper, then a happy, silvery laugh came from her lips.

"Read it to me," said the doctor.

Button read: " 'I, Doctor Hasselton, do hereby prescribe that Mrs. Eric Bjork write me a letter at least once, but better yet, twice a day, until further notice. Doctor Hasselton.'

"Oh, I like that prescription! You can be sure I'll take it as directed. You've made me the happiest person on earth, Doctor."

And it worked! Button couldn't wait for each new day to come so she could write more letters. She wrote one in the afternoon after her walk and very often she wrote a shorter one before retiring. The afternoon letters were more in the form of a report, but the evening ones were of a more dreamy nature.

Afternoon January 10, 19——

Dear Doctor,

I walked today in the snow while the wind whipped my face and the world looked like a huge bowl of whipped cream. (I love whipped cream!) But in spite of the beauty of this winter wonderland, I did not see the snow. No, in my heart it was spring. The first tulips were lifting up their little heads from the dark earth, the lawn had a fine shadow of soft green grass, the leaves were bursting forth on the branches of tree and bush and, of course, hundreds of birds were singing their joyous melodies as they were building their nests! Yes, in my heart spring has come even though the calendar says January, and all because I am getting well. I feel like laughing and singing and having fun. To me this all seems so new that it is almost strange . . . and yet, this is the way I used to feel a long, long time ago . . . and all because of you.

Button

Evening, January 10, 19——

Dear Doctor,

This is just to say good night! I have had such a fine day. I am tired tonight . . . a real honest-to-goodness tiredness and I know that I can go right to sleep. Having been without peaceful sleep for so long, I can really appreciate it now. There is a big silly moon tonight peeking down at me. I wonder, can you see it from your office window and, if you can, does it make you wish you were very young again? (Now that was foolish and perhaps I shouldn't have written it, but I wanted to, so I did. I hope it is included in your prescription!) I will stop now before I say something worse!

Good night,
Button

And the next day:

Dear Doctor,

This is a new day! I am happy because each new day presents a challenge for me to do better, be happier, and send you a better report. It is like climbing a mountain . . . way, way up there is the top for which I am aiming. Sometimes I have almost reached it . . . just a few more steps, and then I tumble down . . . down . . . until the top seems farther away than before. But I shall reach it. One day I shall stand on the summit and shout, 'I made it! I made it!' I know that each tomorrow I shall be better than I was on the yesterday. That assurance I have in my heart, so why should I fear?

Button

Because life commenced to be good again, Button very soon began to feel at home with her family. Sometimes the four of them walked together now, and very often Button would be in a storytelling mood and relate things for the girls from her own childhood. At night, when the girls were in bed, Eric and she often took long rides out through the countryside. She sat close to him and slipped her arm through his and they talked small talk that was gentle and soothing to her spirit and brought them closer together. They spoke of the girls' futures and the things

they would plant in their garden the following spring,
where they would spend their next vacation, anything connected with the daily routine of their homelife. They never
mentioned the past or Button's sickness, and Button never
told of her letters to Doctor Hasselton. A year had gone by
and she still abided by that prescription. To write her letters had become the pattern of her day, a gay pattern, making bright colors in the tapestry of gray.

One day as she was writing her letter, a thought came
to her. She was well now. She really had no need of writing.
Then why did she still keep on? But just the thought of
stopping made her feel as though the sun would stop shining. She hadn't the strength yet to stand alone, she told
herself.

It was marvelous to be well. Her letters were happy
ones now, full of humor and laughter. She did not go to the
doctor's office so often any more; the period between visits
was lengthening.

One beautiful spring night, when she had just mailed
her good-night note to Doctor Hasselton, the question as
to why she was still writing him came to her with an over-
whelming force. Over and over again she asked herself that
question. Did Doctor Hasselton mean more to her than her
own husband? It was a frightening thought and one Button did not like to face. But she did, for honesty had always
been a sacred part of her marriage to Eric. If she was doing
something wrong, she must analyze the situation carefully.
She tossed on her bed that night, thinking of Eric . . . how
dear and fine he was and how hard he had struggled
through those unhappy years. He certainly was entitled to
something better than a wife who lived only for the letters
she could write to her doctor. However, she wasn't unhappy

with Eric, nor was she jealous of Doctor Hasselton's family. What then, had happened to her?

Miraculously the fog around her lifted, and she was out in the clear. She could see distinctly, and she had her answer. . . . Her dream! Her calling! How blind she had been! Writing those letters had fulfilled the dearest desire of her life—to write! Her heart beat wildly with joy. "I have found it!" her heart sang. The doctor had told her there was a reason for her emotional disturbance, and she had found it. It was the neglecting of her talent that had made her ill; it had been dormant for too many years . . . it had ached and cried and sobbed within her and she had not known. She did not need to write letters any more. Her heart was clean. All was well. She would write the final letter to her doctor and give him the glad news.

The morning was utterly beautiful! Eric had gone to work and Charlene and Lynn to school. Button sat a long time at her desk, staring down at the white paper that would soon be filled with words—the last letter to her doctor. The paper was so still, so white, and it drew her like a magnet and slowly her heart followed:

Dear Doctor,
This is the last letter that I shall write to you. For a long time I have known that it was not necessary for me to write, and yet I couldn't bear the thought of not writing you. Why? I kept asking myself. Today I know the answer. Can you understand that I wanted to write to you more than I wanted to eat, or sleep, or live? When I acknowledged that thought, it frightened me. I wondered if it was wrong. Did I like you too much?

It was as if my writing to you was a crutch which I
no longer needed but refused to discard. Then, as bril-
liantly as the sun breaks through the clouds, the answer came to me. Not you, but my love of writing was
the object of my affection. As a little girl I received a
call to write and I gave my dream into God's keeping
that He might give it back to me. But for years I have
neglected my talent; it has lain dormant in my heart,
receiving no consideration, no nourishment, no love,
and it made my body ill. That was the cry I heard at
night, the gloom that was my companion during those
long dark years. Can't you understand it now? You
said we would find it and we have, we have! I shall
never get sick again for I shall write, not letters, but
stories and poems and anecdotes. I can hardly wait to
get started, and I know how happy you are for me. I
still think that you are the most wonderful person that
I have ever known. You did it! Perhaps it is more tangible to see a person get well from a sick stomach, or
to set a broken rib, but to lead a person out of darkness
into light, to heal one's blindness so one can see, that is
more than a cure; it is a miracle. It worried me that I
might be in love with you, but I did not understand. I
never loved anyone but my Eric, and now that I know
this, I can be a better wife to him. I wonder, are there
others who are sick to their souls because they have
lost their dreams, because great talents are slumbering
deep, deep within their hearts? That is your field, Doctor, but I pray my foolish letters may become an instrument for you, a tool by which to dig deep beneath
the surface of something called nerves into the center
that needs healing. I am the fruit of your labor for all
the world to see, and when my first book is written,
you will have had more to do with its production than

anyone will ever know. So here I am, Doctor, happy,
gay and fully recovered!

In deep gratitude,
Button

"Eric," said Button a few nights later as they were sitting hand in hand before the open fire in the living room,
"I'll never be sick again. I've found the cause. It was not the
angel we lost, or Papa's passing away, or the trouble with
Charlene. It was my calling which I pressed down deeper
and deeper. Perhaps you will never fully understand what
I'm trying to tell you, but watch me and see that from now
on I shall be the happiest person on earth. Doctor Hasselton helped me with my problem; it was like a picture puz-
zle not yet put together, but now all the pieces fit and the
picture is whole."

"Then we owe Doctor Hasselton more than we can
ever pay him."

"Yes, darling! We owe him our very happiness. You
see, Eric, life is a trust given to us by God, and we are like a
garden where seed is planted. A seed must either grow or
die. My seed was meant to grow into writing, and it almost died, but fortunately I recognized it with the doctor's
help."

Eric gave Button a puzzled look. "I can't follow you,
dear, but I feel I should sit down and write our doctor a
letter of thanks . . . for getting you back . . . and the
way you are talking, I know you are really back."

Button laughed. "No, Eric, don't write him. Just give
him a ring on the phone. He's a very busy man."

Eric drew her close. "I don't think I'll ever be able to
understand this woman I married. I discover new traits

each day . . . but they don't worry me . . . I like you just the way you are."

That night Button was too excited to go right to sleep; she could feel something stirring and knocking within her and she spoke to it as a mother would to a child.

"Be still, my soul, for out of you shall come, very soon now, a beautiful dream that God has given back to me."

She slept that night with a joyous smile on her lips and with a heart that was happy and content.

CHAPTER 12

❧ The Awaking

It was as though Button had suddenly emerged from the mist into the sunshine. The world was new! Its beauty was breath-taking! Every dewdrop was a miracle as it glittered like a diamond on the roses in the garden. To think that for those many years when she had lived among the shadows she had been blind to the beauty of Eric's roses. Now she waited anxiously for rising time to come each morning so she could stroll through the garden with him before he went to work.

One morning as they stood by the rose bed, Eric cut a red rosebud that was just opening, so exquisite in its beauty that Button thought it must be one of the loveliest of God's creation.

"For you, my dear, from all the flowers in the garden, welcoming you back," he smiled.

"Eric," Button whispered, "Eric, you've learned to say pretty words. That was so lovely I could cry! I feel as if all the flowers, bushes and trees are lifting up their heads and looking wide-eyed, saying, 'Look, our Button is back!' I know they are as happy as you and I. Now we shall live and enjoy every moment of time. By the way, Eric, how many years are left until you are one hundred and eleven?"

Eric laughed. "The same old gal, talking silly as she used to do. But now I like it. Your illness taught me a good lesson, for I never could get used to that other Button, gloomy and cross and without the magic power of dreaming lovely dreams."

"And now, Eric, I shall write. . . . I'll write because I know it is part of God's plan for me. I'll write a book, Eric, but first I'll create a story for our girls, a story of Mama and Papa and our life in the parsonage in Lapland. I'll tell of our coming here, to Berkley Hills, and the new experiences we had in this country. It will be a gay story, full of life, and they will treasure it always and hand it down to their children and their children's children. It could be that years and years from now, Eric, someone will hold up an old manuscript, yellow with age, and say, 'My great-great-grandmother wrote this story way back in the nineteen hundred fifties.' Can't you picture that?"

He drew her close. "I can picture almost anything while you are telling me, but the most important thing is that you are happy. That makes me glad, too. And now may I tell you something about me?"

"About you, Eric?"

"Yes, me. You're not the only one who has dreamed dreams. Believe it or not, I've had a dream for many years. It's not as lofty a dream as yours, for I could never 'hitch my wagon to a star,' but it's a dream just the same. Button, I'm starting my own shop."

Button stared wide-eyed at her husband.

"Eric, oh, Eric, how wonderful! When? . . . How? . . . What? I'm unable to think for a moment. You mean

that you'll have your own machines . . . your own men
. . . not work for anyone else . . . your own place?"

"Something like that, dear. The machines are ordered.
I'm resigning from my job next week, and tonight I want
you to go with me and look over a couple of places I can
rent."

After a happy Eric had driven off and she had blown
him a kiss, Button poured herself another cup of coffee and
sat down on the bench in the garden. The bees were flit-
tering among the flowers, the birds were chirping their
morning songs, and the sun was shining with a new bril-
liance. Her eyes opened wide to drink in all this beauty
and her heart beat fast. To think that she could have been
so unperceptive as to have lived with Eric all these years
and not know that he, too, sheltered a dream. During her
long illness, all through those dark, trembling years, he had
held fast to his dream. And she had thought him incapable
of dreaming! His dream had been different from hers, and
his was on the brink of fulfillment. She was glad! God had
been good to them! As Mama had said, "He does more than
we ask Him to, for he just loves to make us glad!"

These mornings she delighted in getting breakfast for
the girls and watching them go off to school. They were
both blue-eyed blondes, real Scandinavian types. Charlene
was in the last year of high school and would be leaving
home in another year to attend college. How swiftly the
years had flown by! Imagine, little Lynn in junior high.
Soon both the girls would be married and have their own
children. She and Eric would be grandparents! Life offered so many joys, each year a new joy and a new miracle.

Button did not fear the future any more, for in her
heart she knew that she was ready for the dream God was

giving back to her. All she had to do was to commence to write and see her work take shape and form. Now she understood that she had profited from those years of darkness, for she had learned what it was to suffer and to feel lost and bewildered and separated from God. She had gone through life's hard school. Because of this experience her writing would be richer, for she now knew how it felt to walk in the shadows! Once she had heard a voice in her heart saying, "If you can live your dream," and wasn't that living it—to go through joy and sorrow, light and darkness? So in His great plan God can take all the dark yesterdays and turn them into bright tomorrows. She was thankful her suffering was over but glad that she had gone through it, for she had grown stronger because of it, and more mellow in her judgment of others.

Button arose from the garden bench. Today she would start her book for the girls, her Mama and Papa stories. She would use all the talent she possessed, for this would be a trial book out of which her real book would come later. She felt that the words were already in her mind and heart, planted there by God.

There on the kitchen table were the paper and pencil. They drew her like a magnet. She wished Doctor Hasselton could see her now, for she was as happy as when, at this very table, she had written many letters to him. Her gaze wandered out through the kitchen window to the light blue, cloudless sky. . . .

Doctor Hasselton was pleased with her recovery.

"We did it, Button," he beamed, "together we found it! You are cured now for good and need never go backward, just forward to new health and joy and happiness, and someday I shall read that book. Your dream is to create stories. I, too, have a dream, a desire to create whole people. Every doctor has a dream in his heart. Mine has just begun. As you said in your last letter, your illness will serve to help others. I'll always wonder as I deal with people whose nerves are afflicted, if deep, deep down within that person there slumbers another Button . . . someone who has lost a buried dream. I've seen a bit of the mystery of the soul. I know much more now about how to help others."

"I am so very happy," Button smiled. "We all have dreams . . . even Eric. His was strong and practical and tangible, but it followed the same pattern as mine. We call it by different names, perhaps, such as faith or hope or longing, but the foundation of all those yearnings and moods are dreams that knock on the heart and beg to be recognized."

They talked about Eric, and how he had surprised them both.

"Yes, Eric will be a strong dreamer," the doctor said. "I marvel at the courage and strength and fortitude he displayed all through those long dark years. He never lost his sense of balance. You have a man, Button, that many a woman would envy you, for he is kind and has strength of character and will not easily be upset as he sails over life's troubled seas."

"He's like a ship which has an able captain," Button had answered, remembering Papa's words of long ago.

"Yes," confirmed the doctor, "what better definition than that could be given. Eric is a firm, staunch ship that can traverse any ocean."

It had been good to talk to Doctor Hasselton that day.

What a dear friend he had become! How could they ever have succeeded without him?

What an ideal day to begin her story. The girls had left early for a weekend trip with their church group. She and Eric would be alone in their house for the first time in years. As this was Saturday, Eric would be home at noon, but she had the whole morning free and she would use every second of it. There was also the possibility that Eric might telephone her that he wouldn't be home until later in the afternoon, for that happened often these days when he was winding up his work at his place of employment. Now that she knew his secret, she realized why he had spent so much time away from her. Soon now, very soon, he would be his own boss. She also understood now why he had been so happy and relaxed even when very tired, for his dream was coming true. He could visualize it in his mind now and because of this, he was growing in greatness. All was well with his soul, and he would give his time to building stronger and more noble dreams.

Button took one longing look at the paper and pencil, but decided she better put the house in order first. In Charlene's room the bed was made and everything in perfect order. Her older daughter had inherited her grandmother's perfect housekeeping ability. It was different in Lynn's room. Button smiled as she thought of her younger daughter. As much joy and happiness as she created with her sunny disposition, she certainly wasn't tidy. Her room looked as if a cyclone had struck it. Always there was plenty of work to do after her. Charlene never would walk off without helping with the dishes, but Lynn sought for every opportunity to escape from labor. "She will straighten out,"

Button assured herself. Hadn't the many hours of worry
over Charlene as a child turned out to be needless? She was
a fine girl now. Who could say what slumbered in her two
girls' hearts? They too might be dreaming great dreams
for the future. The greatest gift she could give them was
to allow them the freedom to grow up to be themselves.
Their pattern might be very different from Eric's or hers,
for didn't God stamp His own peculiar design on each
heart?

After finishing her work, she wandered once more
through the rooms. It was such a dear house . . . old now
and not sparkling new as in the beginning . . . it had
been lived in with laughter and tears, with songs and sigh-
ings. What precious memories, what many heartaches were
hidden within its walls, serving to endear it to their hearts
more and more with each passing year. The fresh garden
flowers she had picked this morning wafted their fragrance
through the rooms. She would not exchange this home for a
mansion.

The kitchen with its big window overlooking the garden was the nicest room of them all. Now it was summer,
but the view in the fall, when the autumn leaves flaunted
their rainbow colors, would be just as beautiful. In fact, it
was hard to decide which season was the prettiest. Button
loved the spring when the tulips poked up their curious
little funny faces to look at the green world, and the early
summer when Eric's roses burst into bloom. But perhaps
she loved winter best of all, for the snowclad trees and
bushes transformed the yard into a fairy wonderland, reminding her of her own childhood days in Lapland where
winter cold froze all nature into a crisp, magic white world.
Every season had its unique beauty, and she would never

stop being grateful to God for giving them a home such as this. The kitchen was painted yellow and blue, the colors of her homeland flag. The true blue color was that of the Swedish sky mirrored in the hundreds of lakes, and the yellow, she had told the girls, was the exact shade of the ripe grain, ready for harvest, blowing in the wind in the Swedish fields.

Someday, she hoped Eric and she could take the girls to Sweden that they might see and get the feel of their parents' birth land . . . someday when she was an author and Eric a successful businessman! So new dreams were being spun and would be dreamed high until fulfilled.

At last she was ready to start her task. This would have to be a fine story. She must relive it again and again so she could really put Papa and Mama and the parsonage down on paper. Since this book would be her first attempt at real writing, she must open her heart and mind so that everything that was hidden there could pour forth freely.

She let her thoughts wander back. It was spring in Lapland. No place on earth was more beautiful! The leaves on the trees were so fresh and delicate, and in no other place in the world could they be so green, green. The twilight lingered for hours over the mountain until, by the time summer came, there was no darkness at all, just an everlasting day. Oh, she had almost forgotten the beauty of her homeland! The cuckoo bird that called in the treetop, the dark forest, the fields with hundreds of different wild flowers, the little children picking huge bouquets to take home to their mothers. Barefooted they tramped up the road, flaxen-haired and red-cheeked, with laughing blue eyes and chubby brown hands! She had been like that, running barefooted, picking flowers and *smultron*-berries in the ditches. Karin and she had strung those miniature red strawberries on straws and what fun to carry them around to tempt others and finally to sit down on a large boulder and eat them one by one! And the lingonberries! The woods were full of them, and each fall Papa would take them all to pick pails full of them. Button could still smell the sauce as Mama cooked kettles full to store for the long winter and eat with potatoes instead of meat. And the preserve she made to eat especially with *plättar*. . . . Button must recapture all these memories so her girls, too, could live in Sweden while they read the story of her childhood's land.

And so Papa . . . dear, dear Papa! She was in her early teens . . . perhaps it was only thirteen, when they had walked up the mountain on a lovely spring night. What a night! The stars, the moon, and the blue mountains that had looked black that night in the moonlight, the smell of new green leaves, lovers walking arm in arm, soft whispers and silvery laughter all mingled together to make this magic night. The mountains were full of love words . . . and she was walking with Papa. . . . She had had other plans but Papa had said, "Button, I want you to take a walk with me up the mountain road tonight."

When Papa said that, you walked with Papa. He had been very quiet, obviously unaware of the beauty of the night . . . most likely pondering upon his sermon for the following Sunday. Papa received inspiration for his good Sunday sermons by taking long walks. Well, Button was not in the mood to walk quietly. She wanted to talk! She wanted to laugh! She wanted to have fun! She would make Papa talk to her as never before; she would have to or she would scream. So she placed her arm in his and snuggled close. She measured her stride and tried to make it coincide with Papa's long steps.

"It's fun walking!" she said laughingly.

Papa did not answer. He seemed to be totally unaware of her presence.

"Papa," she ventured again. "I've often wondered about you and Mama. How did you happen to marry her when she is so much younger than you?"

Still silence from Papa. He walked fast, looking straight ahead not even glancing at Button. He was quiet for so long that Button thought she must have offended him by mentioning his age. Perhaps he would just ignore her question, for she had been foolish to ask him. Papa was very sensitive and she had wounded his pride.

Then . . . first a chuckle from Papa . . . then he laughed out loud . . . and his arm went around her shoulder.

"Button, my dear," he said, "how I married your Mama . . . that is still a mystery to me. But if you want a story I'll tell it to you."

A story! Papa had been in a storytelling mood and she would never forget the one he had told her. She never knew Papa could be so comical. She laughed more in that one night than she had in a year. And she would write it just as Papa had told it. She would call her story: Thereto I Plight Thee My Troth.

Button wrote with joy! Her pencil flew over the paper. She forgot time and place, and when Eric came home at noon there was no lunch ready for him.

"Oh, darling," she cried, "forgive me . . . I had completely forgotten that I had a hungry husband. I'm having so much fun writing this Papa and Mama story. Oh,

Eric, the girls will love it. They will never have heard of a stranger romance."

Eric frowned, but Button knew it was only to tease her, for behind that frown lurked a happy smile.

"If this is an example of what it is like to have my wife an author, then I will have nothing of it. I shall put my foot down right from the beginning—no lunch—no coffee percolating—just a starry-eyed wife with roses in her cheeks."

"Oh, Eric"—her arms went around his neck—"I am sorry! But as for putting your foot down, you're much too late, Mr. Bjork . . . that foot of yours wouldn't even leave an imprint!"

Soon she had lunch on the table and they discussed the story she was writing.

"Will it be ready for Christmas?" asked Eric.

"I think it will. If I write every chapter as fast as I wrote this first one, it will be ready in a week!"

Day after day Button continued writing until she had four chapters completed. Then she showed them to her friend, Vera Sallin, who was known as a literary critic. Vera read the story with genuine interest.

"This is excellent," she assured Button when she had finished reading it. "Of course there are errors of spelling and construction, but those are not too important and can easily be corrected. I'd be happy to do it for you and at the same time type it for easier reading."

"Oh, thank you, Vera," responded Button with a jubilant face. "I'm so glad you like it! And now I understand what Papa meant about my need for studying. What a fool I was not to continue my schooling in America. How I wish I could undo that big mistake. But it's too late now. You're a dear to help me get the book written correctly so I will not need to feel shame before my girls. Having it typed will make it look like a real book."

Vera finished the work in a week and telephoned Button.

"Come on over, Button. I've something I would like to suggest to you."

Vera had coffee ready when Button arrived breathless with excitement.

"I can't wait to see it, Vera. Does it look like a book?"

They drank coffee in Vera's cozy living room. A heavy rain was beating against the windowpanes, but Vera had a sparkling fire lit in her huge fire place to take the chill from this damp, late-summer day. Button watched the brilliant tongues of fire leap up and down on the big log.

"Button," asked Vera when their coffee was drunk, "have you ever considered what a good book this story would make?"

Button laughed. "You mean that all that foolishness I've written about Papa and Mama should be put into a book for people outside the family to read?"

"Yes, my dear! They would love it! Button, you have a rare gift of making words live on paper. You say things in a simple, natural, home-spun fashion that will fascinate people."

"But if I sold it, I couldn't give it as a gift to the girls at Christmas," protested Button, her heart beating madly.

Vera looked seriously into Button's eyes. "Don't you think the girls would like a real book better?"

Button had never thought of that. It would be wonderful . . . too wonderful for her to grasp.

"Why don't we try to sell it to a magazine first?" Vera

suggested, and she mentioned the name of a prominent magazine.

Button followed Vera's advice. Gently she folded the manuscript and placed it in a large Manila envelope. She enclosed another envelope, self-addressed and stamped just in case . . . if . . . but she would refuse to consider an *if*. She took it to the big mailbox on the corner and deposited it with a prayer.

"Please God," she whispered as she watched it slide down the chute, "please God, don't let them return it to me. Make them accept it . . . please . . . please. If you ever answered a prayer, let it be this one."

Then came the longest wait that Button had ever known. She waited two endless months and three days. Each time she saw the mailman walk up the street she became sick with fear, hoping that he would not produce a large Manila envelope.

Vera was hopeful. "I'm almost certain they'll keep it. If not, you would have heard by now."

"Oh, I do hope they will," sighed Button. "I must learn how to wait patiently, but it is so hard."

One afternoon when she came home from shopping, there it was! It struck her without warning. Right in the door it was, staring at her big as life. Her heart sank and her eyes filled with tears. . . . It couldn't be—but it was. They had sent it back—they didn't want her beautiful story.

It was a hard blow to take. At first it seemed unbearable. She felt as though her dream was lying at her feet bruised and trampled upon, screaming at her for mercy. Mechanically she opened the envelope. Enclosed was a letter from the editor-in-chief—a super-duper rejection letter.

Button's humor, the hominess of her story, her gift of making the characters live were all very fine—*but*. . . . That *but* was such a little word, yet it had the power to upset her whole life. . . . She would just have to do what she had planned from the beginning, give it to her girls. They would love it. Of that she was sure.

Eric found her sitting by the kitchen table her head in her hands and the manuscript before her. He placed his arms around her.

"Oh, Eric," she sobbed while her tears fell freely. "I wish I'd never sent it! I'm crushed now. My heart is broken."

Button wept, clinging to Eric as a drowning person clings to a lifeline. Slowly he released her stranglehold.

"Little one," he comforted as though she was a child, "listen to me. Put that smile back on your lips and that gleam in your eyes. Life hasn't ended because you've met with a disappointment. Don't give up so easily. Some other magazine might accept it. Don't lose heart at the first blow."

Eric was right. She had to go on living. She had to brace herself and try harder. She must start dreaming anew, the same dream.

"I shall never give up, Eric, never, never! Someday your wife will be an author so you had better prepare yourself, Mr. Bjork. I might even become famous! I've just begun, but from now on I shall dream higher and higher ever higher."

He kissed away her tears.

"Fine, Button. I'm proud of you . . . and whatever will be, will be. . . . Let's leave it that way, my dear. I'm sure that any girl who dares to dream the way my wife does will someday see her dream fulfilled."

BOOK IV

CHAPTER 13

With Mounting Wings

Five years might seem long, at times, as they pass down into the history of a human life, but to Button they had been like a golden summer of sunshine and joy. Now as she looked back upon them, she knew that she would love to relive them over and over again. Such unlimited happiness she had never experienced before! Eric's shop was progressing well, causing him to grow younger-looking instead of older. How well she understood the mystery of that, for Eric, too, had a heart overflowing with joy because his dream had been realized.

Yes, many changes had taken place during this span of years. Charlene had married while in her second year of college and Dick, her husband, had become a dear son and had entered into business with Eric. Charlene and Dick had two little boys, so Eric and Button were grandparents at last! She had found that holding two little wiggling fellows in her arms made heaven come upon earth. New dreams were, perhaps, being shaped in Eric's mind. Could

it be that his shop would be passed down to the next gen-
eration? There was something challenging in those
thoughts that Button knew he had each time he gazed into
a pair of dark brown eyes sparkling with life and mischief.
Being grandparents, both Eric and Button had decided,
was a wonderful way, planned by God, to keep you feeling
young.

Lynn was still in college with the world open for any
field of work that she might choose. Button hoped it would
be in the field of religious or social work, something in
Papa's line, serving humanity. However, her popularity
and the number of boys who were weekend visitors made
Button wonder if wedding bells wouldn't end the thought
of a career. Eric shook his head and said that Lynn had
promised him she would finish college before she settled
down with a husband, and he was confident that she would
keep her word.

Mama still lived in her little white bungalow in sunny
Miami. She was getting on in age but lived all alone since
Kerstin, too, was married. She claimed that she liked the
peace and the quiet surrounding her and would live this
part of her life's story in anticipation of the day when she
would be called into the golden sunset and be reunited
with Papa. All her children were married with the exception of Greta, who still preferred the call of a higher education to what she called the drudgery of marriage.

"You see, I shall be like Papa," she laughed when the
family teased her about being an old maid. "After all, he
was forty-three when he married Mama, and she really had
to work awfully hard to catch him at that. I'm going to
have a doctor's degree in education before I even consider
settling down. Also, I'd like to have a trip around the

world, and what man could give me that? I'm going to rent an exclusive apartment where I can just close the door when I want privacy and come and go as I please. Someday I may even buy myself a long sleeky car to hop into when I want to see you all. So, don't feel sorry for me. I'm living the life I want—independent and free."

Well, thought Button, if that is Greta's dream, good luck to her . . . everyone after her own heart's desire! Mama felt that whatever the children did was in God's plan for them and that thought made her very happy. Nim was still a surgeon in Florida and the other three boys had followed in Papa's shoes and were in religious work. Then there was John, Vickey's husband, a minister too. Button knew that Mama must be weaving new dreams into her tapestry of life as she surveyed her great-grandsons, that her highest wish and prayer for them was that they might become ministers as had been their great-grandfather. There was no higher calling unless it was that of being a mother of ministers.

Yes, so very much had happened these past five years, but the greatest of all to Button was the fulfillment of her childhood dream. At this very minute, as she was sitting in her living room, she held the fruit of that dream clasped close to her heart. God had worked in mysterious ways since that Saturday when she had begun her story for the girls, to the present when that story had emerged as a full-fledged book. Button had not recognized that that day had been God's chosen time to give her back her dream . . . that she was ready for it . . . that had been the day of the fullness of time in God's sight.

Her friend Vera had been the instigator of her attempt to write the story not just for her girls but for the whole world to read in a book. Button had been filled with tremendous hope that the first chapter would be sold to a magazine as a story, but she had reckoned without God. The picture was clear now, for that first chapter should not have been printed that way, separated from the rest of the story. Although she had shed many a tear with each subsequent rejection slip from various magazine editors, now she was thankful for them. How shortsighted humans are, she was thinking. God sees clearly far into eternity and He had known it was for Button's best interest not to succeed with those magazines, for if she had, she wouldn't today be hugging this book to her heart.

After many rejection slips, Button had ventured out to give talks on her story—just to small groups at first. If a speaker had at the last minute canceled an engagement, she had willingly filled it. She found that it was almost as much fun to tell stories as it was to write them. That was a gift she also had received from God, a special talent that she had always known she possessed. She recalled that, while she was living in Sweden and was left in charge of the parsonage and the younger children when Papa and Mama were calling on the sick people of the church, she had entertained them and kept them spellbound by her storytelling. In her mind she could see them now sitting, according to size, on the wooden sofa in the parsonage kitchen while she sat on a chair in front of them. She could make up stories quick as a wink. They just came without effort, just the way her writing did. It was, indeed, a precious gift. As she spoke to her groups of people, she would imagine that they were all children sitting on a wooden sofa . . . and she would talk herself right into their hearts.

Often after she had made a speech, people would say

to her, "Have you ever considered what a wonderful book that story would make? Why don't you have it published in book form so we can purchase it?"

Button had smiled her sunny smile. "Perhaps I will someday. If you'll give me your name and address, I'll notify you when that book is ready, and you can buy it from your favorite bookstore."

And she had meant it. She must write that book for all those who wanted her simple PAPA AND MAMA STORIES. The more she spoke before groups, the longer became the list of names until she had so many she hardly knew where to keep them.

Two years had passed since she had begun to write her story. Eric and she again went to beautiful, mountainous New Hampshire for their vacation. As they drove along, Button noticed a sign saying, CAMP FOR THE SOUL.

"Eric," she said, "I like that. Let's stop for a while. Our souls need as much refreshing as our bodies. We've had such a fine time staying in hotels, swimming and climbing mountains, let's make this last part of our vacation different and attend something we know nothing about."

Eric laughed. "My still so unpredictable Button! Where do you get all those crazy ideas that pop into your head? You see a sign and you want to stop. You have no idea what it's all about. A rest for the soul sounds very good, but not to me. I feel cramped and fenced in sitting with crowds of people. Do you know the way I like to worship and get rest for the soul? I like to sit in a rowboat in the middle of a lake, where the hymns are sung by the tiny waves that play upon the keel of my boat. To sit and let the

sunshine beat down upon my bare back . . . to watch the
float . . . I tell you, that is tonic for my soul. . . . When
I pull up my big shiny fish . . . then I feel refreshed."

Button sat still for a moment, trying to find a solution.

"Eric, a voice within me calls me to that camp. I feel I
must go there. I don't like to have us separate . . . but I
can't stand your type of vacation worship. My heart aches
for that poor fish. I think it may be a mother or a father
fish and the children will be orphans . . . and I can't bear
to watch a fish lying in the bottom of a boat gasping for
breath. But if that's what you want, let me go my way for a
couple of days and you go yours, and then we'll both be
happy."

Thus they parted. Eric drove her into the pine grove
where people with shining, happy faces had gathered for a
couple of weeks of spiritual strengthening of their souls.
She found that there was a room she could have so she
kissed Eric good-bye, feeling a little sting in her heart because they so seldom liked the same things.

Button enjoyed the beauty of the lovely spot where
the camp was located; she mingled with kind, gracious
people and gazed at the majestic mountains which stood
guard around the camp. This new experience delighted
her heart. On the second day of her stay, however, news
came over the radio that a hurricane was on the way and
might strike in that vicinity late in the afternoon. Button
did not worry over Eric, for he was very capable of taking
care of himself and would probably seek refuge in the
nearest hotel. All the campers gathered in the large Inn of
the camp where they would stay until they heard that it
was safe to go out again. The leader, a fine young man, suggested that different people entertain the crowd in order to

make the time pass faster. He asked for volunteers. When no one responded, Button, remembering how happy she had made the children at home when she had told them stories, offered her services.

"I can tell a story of How My Mama Got My Papa," she laughed.

Never had she told a story better. She could see her audience relax and forget about the danger that was threatening. Soon they were laughing heartily. By the time she finished, the sun was shining and the hurricane had missed the camp by several miles.

This episode added two hundred names to Button's list of people who wanted her book, if it ever came into being!

Eric picked her up and, their vacation being over, they drove back to Berkley Hills. Life settled down to a regular routine until one afternoon when a very distinguished gentleman rang the door-chime. He introduced himself as a Mr. Warren, and asked Button if she would mind repeating for him the story she had told at a religious retreat in the New Hampshire mountains a few weeks before.

Button bubbled with delight. She was becoming famous for her storytelling! She offered Mr. Warren a cup of coffee and a piece of her delicious cake to eat while he listened to her. Once again she assumed the role of an entertainer and, as she began to speak, she forgot that she had an audience of only one. In her mind she could see the faces of the people at the camp become relaxed and carefree even in the midst of a severe storm, and she fancied she was speaking to them again. As a result, she told her story to Mr. Warren as well as she had told it to them.

"Mrs. Bjork, I hardly know how to thank you. That was a fine performance. I am the manager of one of America's finest and oldest speaking bureaus. Would you consider signing a contract and becoming one of our artists?"

Button couldn't believe her ears! Her eyes twinkled as brightly as stars.

"I would love to," she whispered, wondering in her heart if Eric would mind having her traveling around the country as a lecturer. She hoped that he would understand that this, too, was part of the plan for her life. She must take advantage of this opportunity.

Mr. Warren continued:

"One of our representatives was caught in the hurricane in New Hampshire and drove into that religious camp for shelter. She saw how efficiently you calmed the spirits of those worried people and how expertly you told your story, so as soon as she came back home she called me and said, 'Another star is born!' You will do well with us. Have you ever considered putting that story in a book? Being an author would add to your prestige, Mrs. Bjork."

Button had signed the lecture contract that day and although Eric was a bit disturbed, he would in no way hamper this new Button who had emerged from the shadows into the bright light of day.

"Go ahead," he said. "Someday you'll tire of that hurried, strenuous life, and you'll be very content to stay in your own nest. In the meantime have fun, dear!"

Mama had been surprised, too, and she had written:

All I can say, Button, is, what in the world will you think of doing next! But, of course, I give you my blessing. And remember your Papa was a fine speaker.

He would be proud to know his daughter had the courage to speak to large clubs. God bless you, darling.

And Button had the courage! She spoke to Women's Clubs of all sizes. She traveled far and wide with but one purpose in mind, to make people laugh and be happy. Their laughter was her great reward. People forgot the dangers of atomic bombs and the worry over their children. Button made them believe that God was good and that this world was not such a bad place to live in after all. Each time she returned home she flew into Eric's waiting arms and wondered how she could leave him and her precious home alone for so many days. In the late hours of the night they would sit close together and she would tell him about her trips, and Eric would tell her of the happenings in his business world, of new orders and fine contacts, of a larger demand for products going out. She would bring out her large box of book-order slips and play with them.

"Look, Eric," she would say, "There has to be a book. I can't disappoint this many people."

Step by step she came closer to the realization of her dream. The right people came into her life to help her at the right time. Finally she found an expert literary agent who took over the correcting and selling of her manuscript, and Button devoted her time to her lectures. She lived for the day when she could announce to an audience that her book had been accepted by a publisher. One day the news came . . . the great, great news! Her agent telephoned her to say that one of the country's leading publishers had accepted her story with great enthusiasm. Button thought she would faint with excitement. That moment was so sacred she could hardly bear it. Her heart kept whispering, "Thank you, oh thank you, dear, dear God." After she had been interviewed and photographed by the local newspaper, and friends and strangers alike had called to congratulate her, she wondered if it were all true or if she were dreaming a beautiful dream. There had been a long wait, but now it was a reality . . . it had come to pass . . . her dream had been fulfilled.

She had to laugh at herself when she realized how naïve she had often been, doing foolish things, but wasn't it characteristic of Button to go her own way, ignoring the advice of those who were standing by to help her? She remembered particularly that time in the early spring, when she was walking down Main Street, reflecting upon her own future. Suddenly the thought came to her that she had not informed the local bookstore that she had a book being published. There were only a few months left now before the publication date. She ought to introduce herself to the owner of the store and inquire about an autographing party. Button had no idea that books were sold by the publisher's salesmen but took for granted that each new author would have to promote the sale of her own books. Certainly an autographing party would help, and the local bookstore should be willing to give her one. She decided to visit Mr. Logan and tell him the good news. So she stepped inside the door and inquired for him from the first clerk she met.

"And who may I say is calling?" asked the clerk. "Mr. Logan is a very busy man."

"He probably doesn't know about me yet," confessed Button. "But he will, for I am a new author and have my first book coming out in the fall. Isn't it wonderful?"

The unimpressed clerk had already departed up the stairs in search of the chief executive. In a few minutes she was back, followed by Mr. Logan.

Button smiled her prettiest.

"May I introduce myself? I am Charlotta Bjork of this town, and I have written a book that is coming out this fall. It's my first book, you know. I was wondering . . . you will be selling it in the store, won't you?"

Mr. Logan gave her a curious glare.

"And who is your publisher?" he asked dryly.

Button mentioned the name with pride. It had a transforming effect on Mr. Logan's face, which broke into a smile.

"A very fine publisher, indeed, Mrs. Bjork. You are very fortunate and can feel assured that they will push your book . . . a fine publisher. . . . I wish you much success!"

Mr. Logan grasped her hand warmly. "Very pleased to have made your acquaintance. I presume their salesmen will be around any time now. We surely will order a supply of your books. Thank you for coming in."

Button stared dumbfoundedly at Mr. Logan. This couldn't possibly be all he had to say! Why, he hadn't even invited her into his personal office where he naturally would meet with prominent people. Button hurt with disappointment. She was afraid that at any moment the tears might gather in her eyes, but she took courage and said as she pulled herself up to her full height, "Mr. Logan, I was wondering about the autographing party. Do you have the time now to discuss the matter with me?"

It was Mr. Logan's turn to stare. "The autographing p-party?" he stammered.

"Yes," said Button boldly. Never had she felt more like Mama than at that moment. "Don't you think you ought to give that kind of a party for a local author? It isn't every day that a book is written by someone in your own community."

Mr. Logan smiled kindly, a sad, wistful smile.

"Mrs. Bjork, I can see that you are very new, indeed, as an author, for you have as yet not experienced the suffering of being 'an unknown.' It takes a long time for a new name to become established. We wouldn't dare to buy as many of your books as we would those of a well-known writer . . . but don't despair . . . the time will come . . . but as far as an autographing party is concerned . . . I wish that I could say this kindly or that you would try to understand . . . the last time we had such a party was twenty years ago and that was for a well-known author who had written a fine book. . . . It became a best seller, as I recall it. Only about a dozen of his closest friends came in. . . . Seeing the hurt in his eyes, we disguised our own salesladies as prospective buyers and had them leave the store and then come back in to buy four or five copies of his book . . . just to ease the strain. . . . Autographing parties . . . they are a risky business even for well-known authors."

Button could not believe what she heard. She had counted on a fine time planning the party with Mr. Logan. She had even thought to surprise him by telling about the lists of names she had and offering to turn them over to him for a good start on the sales. His words had spoiled all that. She felt hurt inside and giving him those names might be "risky business."

"Mrs. Bjork," said the bookstore owner, again smiling down upon her and patting her shoulder as if she were a child, "don't look so sad. I wish I could be more encouraging at such a time as this, but I have been in the bookstore business for many years. . . ."

Deeply disappointed she had left the store quickly without a backward glance. She had pictured this meeting so differently. Being an author wasn't as important as she had thought it would be. Button took her time going home. A thought troubled her. How was she to sell hundreds of books if booksellers were not enthusiastic about stocking books from unknown authors? Then characteristically she changed her thoughts. What had she expected! Mr. Logan really had been more than kind and gracious. After all, he didn't know this Charlotta Bjork from Eve. It had been considerate of him to leave his busy desk and talk to her. She must learn not to be ungrateful when a person did his best. Besides, wasn't she forgetting that she had promised to leave everything in God's hands? Hadn't He proved over and over again that He knew what was best for her life? A book was coming out! Her dream had come true! Soon she would hold a book with a jacket on which her name was printed and with pages and pages containing thousands of printed words that she had created. It would sell! It would sell if she was thankful and asked God to bless it.

As she reached her front door, she heard the demanding ringing of her telephone. She hurried to answer it.

"Mrs. Bjork," said a pleasant, slightly familiar voice, "this is Mr. Logan from the bookstore. I've been doing a little thinking. I like your courage and spirited enthusiasm. I believe we'll take the chance and give you a fine autographing party. We'll hope for the best. Drop into the store next time you come downtown and we'll make some plans."

Button was breathless with excitement and the party

had turned out to be a huge success . . . much more so than either she or Mr. Logan ever had anticipated. The bookstore had gone to great lengths to prepare for the event. The store itself had been converted into a lovely parlor with soft rugs on the floor and lounging chairs and flowers everywhere. On the beautifully decorated punch table were large plates of Swedish coffeebread and *pepparkakor*. Seated at the table, one at each end, were her own girls, pouring the coffee. Dressed in their sweet gowns they rivaled the roses on the table in prettiness. Button was sitting behind a long narrow table piled high with books. When she first sat down to autograph the copies, they resembled a high mountain, but they soon dwindled down as the endless line moved quickly before her. Button signed her name hundreds of times and was hugged and kissed and congratulated. Her cup overflowed with happiness and contentment. Representatives were there from the publisher's, and Mama had made the trip all the way from Florida. Pelle, Vickey and John were there and, of course, Eric, looking proud and handsome as he walked around shaking hands with the many people. Button believed he actually enjoyed it!

If Mr. Logan had been worried about not having customers, his worries were needless, for it seemed as if the total population of Berkley Hills had turned out to recognize the new author. The people waited patiently in line to reach the book table. Surely this was the crowning moment of Button's life! Looking at Mama, beaming in the soft chair placed there especially for her, caused Button's heart to beat with joy. Mama was dressed in pink lace and her hair was waved back from her forehead, her eyes could have outshone the stars in the sky, and her smile was as radiant as a summer day. Was it all a dream? If it were, Button prayed that she would dream forever. She felt as if her soul had been lifted with mounting wings above the earth to a golden hill where her heart told her dreams were fulfilled.

Yes, precious memories to be stored in her heart forever! One tender, sacred memory which was already planted there was the memory of Papa, which would blossom as a rare flower to keep her sweet and humble always, for that had been her promise to him.

The week after the autographing party Button and Eric were sitting in the living room talking over the things that had happened to them both—the shop . . . the book . . . the girls—and the future, which now looked bright and promising.

"Eric," said Button, moving close to him on the davenport, "one by one my dreams are coming true. My heart is overflowing with joy and thankfulness . . . burdens and cares seem far away . . . certainly I should be full of sunshine. In spite of all this there is one desire left . . . a yearning deep, deep down in my soul . . . a yearning to go home . . . back to Sweden."

"Well," answered Eric, taking her hand in his, "I see no reason why you shouldn't go back if that is what you want. You have the money for the fare. How does it feel, Mrs. Bjork, to be financially independent of your husband?"

"Oh, Eric," she whispered, disturbed. "Eric, Eric, don't you ever talk like that! I want to be dependent upon you always . . . until the day I die. You have always been overgenerous with me—my own checking account, my own car! I've had so much! I never lacked anything . . . except for that longing in my heart to write . . . and now even that has been filled. We'll pool our money, darling, and do all our planning together. Even if we're fortunate enough to make much money, let's always stay dependent upon each other."

"That was a fine speech, Button, and I quite agree. There's always that fear that you will become so famous you will grow away from me, get beyond my reach. . . . All I ask is that you stay yourself, Button, full of your crazy talk."

"Oh, Eric, Eric, I promise! Is it crazy enough for me to ask that come spring I may board an airplane and fly home to Lapland for a couple of weeks? I want to—to—to . . ." Button's eyes filled with tears and unashamed she let them roll down her cheeks. "Eric, I want to go home and tell Papa."

She reached Lapland at Eastertime on a cold, bleak day. By late morning, while darkness still lingered over the land, Button stood by the big gate, outside the State Church, that lead to the well-kept cemetery. Ever since Mama had come back to America alone, Button had wanted to make this trip. As much as she had ever wanted anything of life, she had wanted to come home to Papa's last resting place . . . to keep a tryst and to make a promise.

Button had flown over the seemingly endless ocean, but the trip had been completed in no more hours than it had taken days when the family crossed from Sweden. The world certainly changes and progresses, thought Button. She had, of course, written to her childhood friend, Karin, and had received an invitation to visit there. Gunnar and

Karin had met her at an airport and they had traveled in Gunnar's comfortable automobile to the Borgesons' lovely villa on the mountainside, a big elegant home that showed every sign of wealth and comfort. They were the parents of five boys, all grown, with the exception of the youngest, who looked at Button with a pair of dark brown eyes that looked exactly like Gunnar's, the way she remembered them. It had been wonderful to see her friends and, of course, she had brought them a copy of her book.

"Button," said Gunnar as they sat at the dining table that first night while a trim little maid served the meal, "you made it! Your dream did come true!"

"Didn't you think it would, Gunnar? Dreams always come true if you dream them high and are persistent enough to dream them until they grow, mature, take shape and form. If you give your dreams to God to keep, they won't get lost in the humdrum of life and at the appointed time they will be given back to you."

Gunnar shook his head. "You still speak in riddles!" He flashed her a sparkling smile. "We're very happy for you, Button."

"Oh, yes, happy and proud," added Karin. "I think this is the most exciting thing I ever heard, and remember, I was with you the day it began . . . right when the dream started. Remember the day you wore that pretty apron?"

"Yes, Karin, and you thought I remained so long in front of the class because I wanted to show it off . . . and have you forgotten that deacons' meeting?"

"Hey, girls," protested Gunnar laughingly, "you're leaving me behind. . . . I can't follow you . . . I never heard of those episodes . . . if I had, perhaps I never would have dared to marry Karin."

Button joined in the laughter, but she couldn't help feeling that there also were many things that she and Gunnar could speak of, that only they two knew. Never, now, would they mention these things to each other. Nevertheless, they were spun into the fabric of their lives.

How pleasant the visit was and how enchanting to wander back to the old familiar scenes! Yet many changes had taken place as this small mining town had prospered and progressed. Button had only a few days to stay here before returning home and she was not sorry because she knew that her heart belonged with her loved ones in her wonderful America.

"I'll drive you to the cemetery tomorrow morning," said Gunnar the night before Easter. "I don't know why you insist upon going at daybreak, but I do know it is too far for you to walk."

"Thanks, Gunnar, but would I be presuming too much, if I asked to borrow your car and drive myself there? Please forgive me . . . but when I enter that cemetery, I'd like to be alone."

And Gunnar had understood.

Now she stood in the cemetery as the first rays of the sun touched the cold tombstones. Slowly Button began her walk between the graves. Mama had given her explicit directions so she had an idea where that certain stone for which she was looking stood. As she walked, she thought of the first Easter morning and of the woman who had also walked to a grave. The mystery of the morning captured her imagination. The birds were singing now and she breathed deeply of the fresh mountain air. Around her was a heavy, dewy fragrance. . . . All was quiet and peaceful here among the dead. Here in this little cemetery so far away from the noisy world people slept their final sleep. These people had lived and dreamt and watched the sun rise as she was doing, and now their bodies rested in the peaceful soil of their homeland while their spirits were home with God. Here she was searching for Papa, but she knew he was not here . . . only a stone to mark the place where his body had been laid to rest. Papa was far beyond the cemetery in the safekeeping of God's golden eternity. He lives forever! That message he had preached all those many years.

Now she had reached her destination. Reverently she approached the grave and stood there for a moment, her head bowed in prayer and her hand resting on the stone. A sunbeam gleamed upon a name. She read the inscription carved upon the stone:

HÄR VILAR PASTOR PONTUS FRANZON
Född 1867
Död 1938
(sov gott Papa lilla)

How like Mama to have added that extra sentence. Translated it read, "Sleep well, Papa dear."

How long she remained in the cemetery, Button did not know, but she spent a long time talking with God, thanking Him for a father like Papa, for the wisdom and love he had planted in her heart, and even for the discipline he had enforced to mold into her a strong character. Before she left, she knelt down on the cold ground and lifted her face toward the sky.

"Papa," she whispered as the bright tears shimmered in her eyes, "I know that you're not here, but this is the place where your dear body was laid to rest. This Easter morning I want to make a pledge to you and a promise that I will follow in the faith that you gave me . . . that I will live as you taught me . . . and that the memory of you will always keep me humble, realizing that all good things are gifts from God. Papa, many a promise to you I broke in my childhood. I caused you much trouble and heartache, but, Papa, I've come all the way from America back here to tell you that Button has turned out all right and you can be proud of her now."

So she left him there and part of her heart with him, and flew back home again to Eric, Lynn, Charlene and Dick and their boys. She was richly blessed to have all these to hold and love forevermore.

Charlene had met her at the airport in New York.

"I had to come all the way, Mommie, to be the first one to greet you. I wouldn't even let Daddy come with me for I have such good news, Mommie. There's going to be another baby . . . in September . . . your month . . . perhaps another author . . . who knows?"

Button drew her close.

"I'm so happy, darling, so happy! But how many children are you going to have? Three is quite a handful!"

Charlene laughed. "I just love having babies, Mommie! I sometimes think that I may have as many as Grandma Franzon. Perhaps they'll say it's inherited! I just can't imagine not having a little baby in the house."

Yes, Charlene indeed resembled Mama and life seemed to follow a pattern. Hadn't Mama received the news when she returned from Sweden that she was to have a grandchild? . . . Only this was Button's third. Yes, indeed, she was blessed!

It was another morning and the world was fresh and new. Button's eyes were wide as she beheld the wonders in her garden and listened again to the happy chirping of the birds as they built their little nests. She had just waved good-bye to Eric and the smile was still on her lips for Eric had asked, "What is that that you hold so tightly to your heart?"

And she had responded, "Dirt, Eric, just plain garden dirt."

"And why the box, Button?"

"That's such a long story that, if I were to tell you, you'd never finish that gauge today . . . so good-bye, dear."

Eric had laughed. He probably thought that this was just some new crazy thing Button had thought up . . . to carry around with her a bit of dirt in a box.

Button walked to the tulip bed and gazed down upon the profusion of colors. Soon the lilies of the valley would be in bloom and the lilac was budding. She almost worshiped this plot of land Eric and she had made into a beautiful garden. The love of one's land! she thought. There is where your heart takes root and that was why she wanted to share with it a most precious gift, the gift Karin had given her when she left Sweden.

"It is Sweden!" Karin had said. "You can hold it between your fingers and say, 'I am home!' "

Slowly Button emptied her box among the flowers. She saw the dirt spill over the leaves of the tulips, gray dark dirt that once had contained seeds in her homeland.

She had known she would do this ever since she had said good-bye to her friends after leaving Papa's grave. When she had first come to America, she believed that no matter how carefully she tried to pull up her roots, a few would remain in the land of her birth. . . . Those few roots had called her back . . . but now that she had kept her tryst with Papa, those last roots had been severed.

Over to this great land in the west people had come. Immigrants they were called, whose hearts were weeping with loneliness for the land they had left. But they pressed onward until they knew they were claimed by the new land. They learned that they belonged, not back in the yesteryears or in the land that gave them birth, but in the adopted country whose arms had been open wide to give them a mother's sheltering love.

Button could visualize the long procession of wanderers who had found their homes here. And wasn't this nation's greatness built upon this love the wanderers carried with them from their home soil and planted over here? She was proud to be one of these people, for she loved this land which had fulfilled her heart's desire.

Gently her fingers touched the dirt and together with a tear that rolled from her eye, she mixed it with the garden soil.

"To my new beloved country," she heard herself say aloud, "as a gift from Papa's daughter."

As Button's eyes swept over the horizon, a smile came to her lips, for she knew that her heart had found peace and that her roots had dug themselves deep into the rich soil of her new homeland.